Rival Riders Rising

A Teen Equestrian Friendship Drama About Competition, Courage, and the Medal Finals

The Saddle Creek Riders

Book 3

Wren Willowbrook

Chapter One

Emma Parker had always believed that mornings at Saddle Creek felt different from any other morning anywhere else. They felt fuller, warmer, brighter somehow, even when the sun had barely climbed above the barn roof. Today was no exception. The air smelled like fresh hay and leather, and the soft nickering of sleepy horses drifted from every stall as she crossed the yard toward the tack room.

Willow poked her head over her door the second she spotted Emma. Her silvery chestnut coat glowed even in the cool light, and her dark eyes softened happily. Emma paused, pressed her forehead gently to Willow's, and let the mare's breath warm her skin. For a moment, everything in the world felt exactly right.

"You knew I was coming," Emma whispered. "You always do."

Willow shifted her weight as if saying of course, and Emma laughed softly, the tension she did not even know she carried easing from her shoulders. The mare had been her anchor through everything, from the first chaotic weeks at Saddle Creek to the wild, emotional mystery with the injured foal in the woods. Even now, months later, she still felt a little flutter in her chest thinking about how far she and Willow had come.

Emma brushed a strand of windblown hair from her face and glanced toward Knightfall's stall across the aisle. The tall bay gelding stood quietly, ears flicking toward her. Something about him made her pause. His eyes seemed heavier than usual, almost thoughtful. Or maybe she was imagining it. Knightfall was steady and calm, the kind of horse who noticed everything but reacted only when he needed to.

Still, as Emma watched him, he shifted his hind leg and gave a tiny flick of his ears, like he was listening to something far away.

"You okay, boy?" Emma murmured across the aisle.

Knightfall blinked slowly, but he did not step forward or stretch his neck toward her the way he usually did when she said hello.

She tucked the thought away for later. There was no reason to worry, she told herself. Riders sometimes read too much into small things. Coach Sloane said that all the time. Knightfall was probably fine. Or maybe he was just sleepy.

Emma forced a small smile and stepped toward the tack room, her boots crunching on the thin layer of frost coating the gravel. The weather had turned sharply colder this week, and everyone at the barn had been whispering about the first snow being close. The idea of winter felt distant last month, but now... it was coming fast.

She pushed open the tack room door, expecting to find the usual early-morning quiet. Instead she froze.

Every rider at Saddle Creek seemed to be gathered there, crowded around the bulletin board. Jackets brushed against each other. Winter hats bobbed. Boots squeaked on the rubber mat. Voices buzzed excitedly. Even Coach Sloane stood at the front, arms folded, a rare smile lighting up her usually serious face.

Emma's heart skipped. Something big was happening. She could feel it.

Riley spotted her first. Her blond braid was crooked and her cheeks pink from rushing, but her grin was wide.

"Emma, hurry up. You're missing it."

"Missing what?" Emma squeezed between Harper and Zoey to get closer to the board.

Harper's eyes were wide behind her glasses. "Coach Sloane just put up the new winter competition schedule."

"And there is something huge on it," Riley added dramatically. "Huge."

Zoey nodded, though she said nothing. She held her gloves tightly in both hands, twisting them slowly. Emma noticed the tension in her shoulders and made a mental note. Zoey had been quieter lately, almost withdrawn since the foal rescue ended. Emma planned to talk to her later, but right now Zoey was focused on the bulletin board.

A new poster, freshly printed and perfectly centered, gleamed under the tack room lights:

SADDLE CREEK EQUESTRIAN
WINTER YOUTH MEDAL CLASS
AGES 13 TO 16
QUALIFIERS BEGIN THIS MONTH

Emma's breath caught.

"A medal class?" she whispered.

Coach Sloane stepped forward. "This winter, the region is launching a brand-new medal series. Saddle Creek is one of the host barns. It is a stepping stone for serious riders who want to build competition experience. Riders who qualify will compete in the winter medal finals."

Riley gasped. "Like a real final? With judges and ribbons and everything?"

Coach Sloane nodded. "One of the biggest youth regional events of the year."

Emma felt something warm and fluttery rise inside her chest. A new medal class. Something designed for riders like her, Riley, Harper, Zoey. Something that could help them improve, maybe even shine. Potential shimmered in the air like frost.

But then Coach Sloane kept speaking, and Emma felt the energy shift.

"For this series, you will not be riding your usual lesson horses every week. We will be assigning mounts based on skill level and horse availability."

Emma's heartbeat stumbled. For months, Willow had been her constant partner. They trusted each other, understood each other, and grew together. The idea of riding another horse for the medal class made her chest tighten. She knew she would have to learn to ride other horses eventually, but she had hoped it would be later, not now.

Riley elbowed her gently. "You okay?"

"I think so," Emma said, though she was not entirely sure. "It will be fine. Right?"

Riley was quiet for a moment. Unusual for her. Then she nodded. "Yeah. I mean... yeah. It will be good. Coach says it's normal in big shows. We can do it."

Harper shifted uncertainly. "Do you think she'll put us on unfamiliar horses? Because I am still figuring out Chase. And he likes to pretend shadows are monsters."

Emma smiled. "He only did that once."

"Three times," Harper corrected.

Zoey stared at the poster, saying nothing. Her fingers twisted her gloves tighter.

Coach Sloane cleared her throat. "There is more."

Riley whispered loudly, "There is always more."

"This winter," Coach Sloane said, "we will also be hosting a special clinic. A three-day intensive training event. A guest trainer will be coming to Saddle Creek."

Harper's mouth dropped open. "A guest trainer? Like... famous?"

"Very experienced," Coach Sloane replied, giving her a small smile. "And very honest. You will need thick skin."

Riley exchanged a look with Emma. "Very honest sounds terrifying."

Emma laughed softly. "Maybe it will be good for us."

Coach Sloane continued, "The clinic will take place during the first big snow of the season. That means most of our riding will be indoors. Be prepared for the limitations of winter training. Space will be tight and tempers may flare."

Zoey's eyes flicked nervously between Coach Sloane and Riley.

Emma noticed it instantly. Something was brewing under the surface. Something small now, but not forever. She stored it away in her mind, the way she always did when she sensed tension between her friends.

Coach Sloane tapped the medal class poster. "For now, I want each of you to focus on the qualifiers. This is an opportunity for every one of you. Saddle Creek has a chance to make an impression this season."

Emma felt her pulse quicken. She wanted this. She wanted to try. Not to win, not yet, but to grow. To learn. To ride with confidence. To show that she and Willow were becoming a stronger team, even if she could not always ride Willow in every competition.

The room buzzed with questions. Riley asked whether dress code rules were changing. Harper wanted to know how the courses would be designed. Zoey asked quietly if the qualifiers were open to spectators. Emma stood back, letting the wave of excitement wash over her.

Then Coach Sloane said something that made several riders freeze.

"Oh, and one more announcement. We will be welcoming a new student this week. A boy rider. He is transferring from another barn and will be joining your age group."

The air changed instantly.

Riley blinked. "A boy? Here?"

Emma frowned. "Why does that matter?"

Riley shrugged. "It is just different. We never have new students our age. And never boys."

Harper adjusted her glasses. "Do you think he is nice?"

Zoey looked down. "Or talented?"

"Or both," Riley muttered grimly.

Emma did not know what to think. A new rider could mean anything. A new friend. A new rival. A new energy in the barn. Change was not always bad. But it was rarely simple.

Coach Sloane started handing out practice schedules while everyone whispered guesses about the new rider. Emma accepted her sheet distractedly, her mind spinning.

A new medal class. A winter clinic. A new rider. Indoor riding. Tight spaces. Rising tension.

And somewhere behind all of it, Knightfall's quiet, thoughtful eyes lingered in her memory, as if he had been trying to tell her something earlier.

She pushed the thought aside again, but less confidently this time.

The meeting dissolved gradually until the riders filtered back toward the main barn. Emma stayed behind for a moment, staring at the poster, her fingers tracing the bold letters at the top.

Winter Youth Medal Class.

She imagined herself jumping a clean round, Willow watching proudly from the rail, Coach Sloane nodding in approval. Her heart soared. She wanted this. More than she had expected.

Riley swung an arm around Emma's shoulders. "We are going to crush this medal class. I mean, crush it."

Emma laughed. "You have not even seen the course yet."

"I do not need to," Riley replied confidently. "I just know we are going to be amazing."

Harper smiled softly at them. "I am excited. And nervous. But mostly excited."

Zoey lingered behind them, her expression unreadable.

Emma nudged her gently. "What about you?"

Zoey hesitated. "I... I think it is a lot. A new class. A new rider. A clinic. Indoor season. I do not know. It feels overwhelming."

Emma nodded sympathetically. "It is okay to feel that way. We will get through it together."

Zoey gave a small, grateful smile, but it did not reach her eyes fully.

When the girls reached the barn aisle, Willow greeted Emma with a soft whicker. Knightfall lifted his head too, though more slowly. Emma could not shake the strange feeling from earlier, so she walked over to him.

"Hey, Knightfall," she whispered. "You doing alright today?"

The gelding shifted again, almost subtly, and let out a small breath.

Emma pressed her palm gently to his shoulder and felt a slight stiffness under her hand. Not much. Barely noticeable. But it was real.

She frowned. "You are sure you are okay?"

Knightfall nuzzled her sleeve, sweet as always, but something in Emma's chest tightened. It was like a tiny warning bell ringing faintly from somewhere far away.

She told herself it was nothing. Just imagination. Just nerves from the news.

Still, she glanced back toward the bulletin board, toward the medal class announcement, the clinic poster, and the new rider rumor swirling through the barn.

Change was coming to Saddle Creek. Big change. She could feel it in the air, crackling like frost before a storm.

Emma took a breath, straightened her shoulders, and reached for Willow's halter.

Whatever this medal season brought, she would face it.

She just hoped her friends would stay close, that Willow stayed confident, and that Knightfall's strange stiffness was nothing more than a one-morning fluke.

Because deep down, somewhere under all the excitement, Emma sensed that this winter at Saddle Creek was going to challenge them in ways none of them expected.

And it was only beginning.

Chapter Two

The following afternoon, Saddle Creek hummed with a nervous kind of energy. It was not the usual after-school rush, or the cold snap settling over the property, or even the talk about winter qualifiers. It was something sharper. Livelier. The kind of buzz that meant news was spreading faster than it could be confirmed.

The new rider was arriving.

Emma heard at least four different versions of the story before she had even finished brushing Willow. According to Riley, he was a hotshot jumper from a competition barn down south. According to Zoe from the beginner class, he had placed in three regional circuits already. According to a tiny first-year student named Molly, he rode a wild stallion with glowing eyes, which Emma highly doubted. And according to Harper, he was probably just a normal kid who wanted to ride.

Emma hoped Harper was right. Saddle Creek was small, friendly, and close-knit, which made new arrivals feel enormous. The last time a rider transferred in, it had taken months for everyone to adjust. Emma would know. She had been that rider.

She tightened Willow's girth and ducked under the mare's neck to check the other side. Willow breathed softly, warm air brushing against Emma's cheek. It steadied her more than she wanted to admit.

"I do not know why everyone is acting like this is the Olympics," Emma whispered. "It is just one rider."

Willow flicked her ears as though she agreed.

Riley appeared suddenly at her stall door, nearly vibrating with energy. "He is here."

Emma blinked. "Already?"

"Yes. Now. This very second," Riley said, hopping from foot to foot. "He is unloading in the parking area with Coach Sloane."

Harper poked her head around the aisle corner. "She means they are walking in. I saw them from the hay loft window. He looks serious. And tall."

Zoey stood a little behind Harper, clutching her helmet. "What if he is one of those riders who thinks he is better than everyone?"

Riley shrugged. "Then we prove him wrong."

Emma shook her head, pulling the saddle pad straight. "Let us not decide anything before we meet him."

But she felt a tiny, fluttering uncertainty inside her stomach. A new rider meant change, and change always shifted the barn's balance. Sometimes for the better. Sometimes not.

Riley tugged on Emma's sleeve. "Come on. We have to see him before the lesson starts."

"Riley," Emma protested lightly, "we should tack up first."

"We have ten minutes," Riley insisted. "Ten. Minutes. That is basically a lifetime."

Emma laughed despite herself. "Fine. But only for a minute."

They hurried down the aisle toward the main entrance, Harper and Zoey following closely. The sounds of boots on gravel and muffled voices drifted in from outside. Riley skidded to a stop just before the door and peeked out dramatically.

"Oh," she breathed. "There he is."

Emma moved beside her and looked.

The boy stood near Coach Sloane, holding a black riding helmet loosely at his side. He was tall for their age, with dark, slightly messy hair and sharp, observant eyes. He wore a charcoal jacket and crisp riding pants, the kind Emma usually saw only at shows.

But it was not his clothes that caught her attention.

It was the way he carried himself.

Confident. Focused. Like someone who had spent years in structured training and knew exactly where he was going.

Coach Sloane was speaking, pointing toward the barn. The boy nodded once, listening intently.

Riley elbowed Emma. "He looks... good."

"Good?" Emma whispered.

"I mean good at riding," Riley said quickly. "He looks very capable. And possibly extremely annoying."

Harper cleared her throat quietly. "We should be polite."

Zoey nodded, though her face showed nerves creeping in. "Maybe he is nice."

Riley snorted softly. "He is not even inside yet and Emma already looks worried."

"I do not look worried," Emma said automatically, though she kind of did feel something tightening in her chest. "I just hope he fits in."

Coach Sloane led him through the open doorway, and the four girls stepped back instinctively.

"Girls," Coach Sloane said, her tone warm but firm, "this is Cade Lawson. He will be joining your intermediate group starting today."

Cade inclined his head in a small greeting. "Hi."

Riley stared at him like she was evaluating his entire soul. Harper gave a shy wave. Zoey murmured a hello so soft Emma almost missed it.

Emma offered a friendly smile. "Welcome to Saddle Creek."

Cade looked at her for a moment, unreadable, then nodded. "Thanks."

His voice was calm. Courteous. But distant.

Coach Sloane continued, "Cade comes from Clearwater Ridge, a competitive barn in the southern region. He has experience with jumpers and equitation and has competed at several schooling circuits."

Riley's eyebrows shot up. "So he is good."

Coach Sloane gave her a look. "Skill is important. Attitude is more important. He is here to work hard and learn the way we do things."

Emma felt Harper relax slightly beside her.

Coach Sloane looked at the riders. "Since you all have your lesson together today, I want Cade to start on one of our steady horses so he can get used to our style." She glanced toward the far stalls. "I am assigning him to Knightfall."

Emma's eyes widened. "Knightfall?"

Cade looked up with interest. "That is the bay gelding? I saw him on the walk in. He looks solid."

"He is," Coach Sloane replied. "He is also sensitive and responsive. Treat him with respect and he will meet you halfway."

Cade nodded once. "I can handle that."

Emma swallowed. She could not explain it, but Knightfall had never been assigned to a brand-new rider in their age group before. Ever. He was picky in small, subtle ways. He liked calm hands, patient cues, and riders who gave him time to think. And lately, Emma sensed something off in him. Nothing huge, just... different.

She wondered if Coach Sloane knew that too.

Maybe Cade needed a horse like Knightfall. Or maybe Knightfall needed a rider who would not push him too hard.

But Emma still felt a strange twist in her chest. Knightfall had always been special, even if he was not her own. Seeing him assigned to someone new felt odd.

Coach Sloane clapped her hands lightly. "Everyone finish tacking your horses. The lesson begins in ten minutes."

Riley moved first, shooting Cade a lingering glance. Harper gave him a small, friendly smile before hurrying after Riley. Zoey looked down, whispered something like welcome again, and walked off quietly.

Emma stayed for a moment longer.

Cade set his helmet under his arm. "So. That is Knightfall's stall?" He nodded toward the far end.

"Yes," Emma said. "He is gentle, but he likes riders who listen to him. He is very smart."

Cade's eyebrows raised slightly. "Horses like when you listen. All of them."

Emma blinked, not sure whether that was an agreement or a correction. "Right. I just meant he can be particular."

He shrugged. "Most good horses are."

Emma did not know how to respond. Cade's tone was not rude, exactly. More like matter-of-fact, as if he was speaking a universal truth she should already know.

She stepped aside. "Good luck in the lesson."

"Thanks," he said, already moving toward Knightfall's stall.

Emma turned and walked quickly back to Willow, her heart beating faster than it should. She could not figure out whether Cade was confident or arrogant. Helpful or blunt. Quiet or aloof.

Riley's voice echoed in her memory.

He looks very capable. And possibly extremely annoying.

Emma was not sure she agreed. At least not fully. But she also was not sure she disagreed.

She grabbed her helmet and fastened her girth, brushing Willow's shoulder where the mare liked to be scratched.

"You are the best girl," Emma whispered. "No matter what changes around here."

Willow leaned into the touch, steady and loyal as ever.

As Emma led Willow toward the arena, she saw Cade entering the opposite end with Knightfall. He walked with long, confident strides, shoulders squared, reins draped lightly in his hand. Knightfall followed calmly enough but flicked an ear backward, not fully relaxed.

Emma frowned faintly.

Something still felt off about Knightfall.

She hoped it was nothing. She hoped he was just adjusting to the cold.

The lesson began with simple warm-ups. The riders walked their horses in a large circle. Coach Sloane called out instructions with crisp clarity.

"Long reins and forward walk. Keep your eyes up. Let your horses loosen their backs."

Emma rode Willow in a steady rhythm, her seat warm against the saddle, each footstep soft and even. Harper guided Chase carefully along the rail, keeping him away from a suspicious patch of sunlight. Riley circled Ember with confident hands, though the mare was feeling energetic and kept tossing her head.

Zoey rode Daisy, quiet and composed, though she kept glancing toward Cade and Knightfall.

Emma tried not to watch, but she could not help it.

Knightfall walked obediently beside Cade. The boy's posture was straight, his hands steady. He looked comfortable. Natural, even. He was not gripping with tense legs or overcorrecting the reins. For a newcomer, he seemed to integrate smoothly into the rhythm of the class.

Coach Sloane observed him for a while, then turned her attention back to the group.

"Pick up a trot. Maintain spacing. Control your corners."

The arena echoed with hoofbeats. Emma urged Willow forward, feeling the familiar bounce of the trot beneath her. She relaxed her hands and settled into the rhythm.

Out of the corner of her eye, she saw Cade post effortlessly. Knightfall's head bobbed evenly, his stride long and fluid.

Maybe Emma had worried for nothing. Maybe Knightfall was perfectly fine. Maybe he was just reacting to the cold this morning, nothing more.

But then, as the riders changed direction, Emma saw something subtle.

Knightfall hesitated.

Just for a moment. A fraction of a second. Cade asked for a corner bend, and Knightfall took an extra step before responding.

It was small. Almost invisible.

But Emma saw it.

And a flicker of unease returned.

Coach Sloane called out, "Prepare for your first canter transition."

Riley grinned. "Finally."

Emma steadied her reins, deepened her seat, and asked Willow for the canter. The mare responded beautifully, lifting into a smooth, rolling gait that warmed Emma from the inside out.

She let Willow stretch, her mane waving gently. The cold air rushed past her face, carrying hints of snow.

Harper cantered Chase in small, careful circles. Zoey guided Daisy with quiet concentration. Riley raced a bit too enthusiastically, earning a stern look from Coach Sloane.

Cade asked Knightfall for the canter.

The gelding hesitated again.

Just half a stride. Barely noticeable.

Then he moved into the gait, elegant and steady.

Coach Sloane did not seem to notice the tiny delay. Maybe Emma was imagining it. Maybe she was looking too hard.

But the moment stayed with her.

After several minutes of cantering, Coach Sloane signaled for them to return to a walk. The class lined up in the center.

"Good warm-up," she said. "Now let us work on poles and small crossrails. Riders, begin at the trot. Focus on straightness and rhythm."

As the poles were set, Riley leaned toward Emma and whispered, "He is pretty good."

Emma nodded reluctantly. "Yeah."

"I mean, I do not like him yet. But he is good."

Emma smiled faintly.

When it was Cade's turn, he guided Knightfall toward the poles with steady confidence. The gelding pricked his ears, stepping lightly.

He cleared the poles smoothly.

Coach Sloane nodded. "Good. Give him more release next time."

"Yes, Coach," Cade said.

Emma found herself surprised again. Cade listened. He took feedback seriously. He was not bragging or showing off. He was just riding.

The lesson continued with small crossrails, then slightly higher ones. Willow stayed consistent. Ember grew excited. Chase tried to avoid one colorful pole. Daisy tripped once but recovered.

And Knightfall...

Knightfall jumped well.

Mostly.

But Emma kept noticing the small delays. The subtle reluctance. The way his ears flicked back for a split second before taking off. He was not refusing. Not rearing. Not balking. But something was not fully right.

Cade did not seem to notice. Or if he did, he did not show it. His confidence never faltered.

When the lesson ended, Coach Sloane clapped her hands. "Cool down your horses and untack. Good work today."

The riders dispersed.

Riley rode up beside Emma. "Okay. He is good. But I still think he is hiding something."

"Hiding what?" Emma asked.

"I do not know. Something."

Emma rolled her eyes affectionately. "You always think someone is hiding something."

"Not always," Riley said, then paused. "Okay. Maybe most of the time."

Harper joined them, smiling. "He seems nice. Quiet, but nice."

Zoey, walking Daisy, whispered, "He did not talk to anyone during the break."

Emma shrugged. "Maybe he is nervous. It is his first day."

Cade dismounted near Knightfall's stall and loosened the girth. Coach Sloane spoke with him briefly, pointing out a few details about Knightfall's care. Cade listened attentively.

Emma led Willow past them, and Cade looked up.

"Your mare is pretty," he said.

Emma blinked. "Thank you. Her name is Willow."

"Nice movement," Cade added. "She looks willing."

Emma was not sure whether that was a compliment or just an observation. But she smiled anyway. "She is."

Cade nodded slightly, adjusted Knightfall's reins, and led the gelding into his stall.

Riley muttered under her breath, "He compliments horses like he is judging a show."

Emma whispered back, "Do not overthink it."

Riley crossed her arms but did not argue.

As Emma brushed Willow's coat after the ride, she thought about everything that had happened. Cade seemed talented. And serious. And maybe a little intimidating. But not unkind. Not yet.

Still, her thoughts kept drifting back to Knightfall.

His hesitation. His slight stiffness. The small moments Coach Sloane had not seen.

Maybe it really was nothing.

Or maybe Knightfall was trying to tell them something.

Emma ran her hand down Willow's shoulder, feeling the mare's warmth beneath her touch.

"Tomorrow will tell us more," she whispered.

Outside, wind rattled the barn roof gently.

Snow was coming.

Change was coming.

And Emma had a feeling that this winter was going to test all of them, starting with Knightfall.

Chapter Three

By the next morning, frost sparkled across every fence rail at Saddle Creek, turning the barn into a world of silver and blue. Emma arrived early enough that the fields still lay quiet, the sun not yet strong enough to melt the thin white crystals blanketing the grass. Her breath puffed into the air, forming small clouds as she hurried across the yard.

Today's lesson mattered.

Coach Sloane had said they would start medal class preparation. That meant more technical exercises. More precision. More pressure. And, for Emma, a chance to show that yesterday's nerves about Cade had been nothing more than first-day jitters.

She hoped everyone would settle into their usual rhythms.

But as she approached Willow's stall, she noticed Knightfall first.

The tall bay gelding stood completely still, ears tilted back just slightly, eyes soft but... watchful. He was eating, but slowly. Methodically. As if each bite required thought.

Emma felt a tiny pinch of worry she tried to swallow down.

"Morning, Knightfall," she whispered.

He lifted his head and nickered, but the sound lacked its usual enthusiasm.

Before she could step closer, Cade appeared, walking briskly from the tack room with Knightfall's bridle swinging lightly in one hand.

He looked rested. Focused. Like someone who had already made a checklist for the day.

"Hey," Emma said quietly. "Morning."

Cade gave a short nod. "Morning."

He slipped into Knightfall's stall with measured confidence. Knightfall lifted his head again, flicked an ear, and shifted his weight.

Emma watched from across the aisle, brushing Willow's neck as she observed the pair. Cade worked efficiently, checking the bridle with practiced ease. His hands moved with confidence, but Emma noticed he kept a firmer contact on Knightfall's head than she would have. The gelding accepted it without complaint, but something in his posture tightened.

Willow nosed Emma's sleeve, drawing her back to her own horse. The mare's warm breath grounded her again. She focused on tacking up, careful and methodical, but her mind wandered to the lesson ahead.

Riley arrived next, stomping frost off her boots. "Okay," she declared dramatically. "I have decided. Cade is either going to be a problem or a good surprise. No in-between."

Emma laughed. "That covers every possibility."

"Exactly." Riley nodded with exaggerated seriousness. "I like to be thorough."

Harper followed behind her, adjusting her helmet strap. "I think he is just quiet. Not rude, not bossy. Just quiet."

Zoey joined them silently, Daisy trailing behind her on a lead. She did not add anything to the conversation.

Emma paused, studying Zoey for a second. She looked tired. Or maybe overwhelmed. Her shoulders sank slightly as she stroked Daisy's nose.

Emma made a mental note to check on her later.

But before she could say anything, Coach Sloane walked into the aisle, brisk with purpose. "Good morning. Saddled and ready, everyone? We are in the outdoor arena today. The footing is firm enough and the cold will help your horses stay alert."

"Alert," Riley repeated. "Great."

Emma led Willow out alongside the others, cold gravel crunching under their boots. The morning sunlight cast long shadows across the yard, illuminating the soft plumes of breath rising from each horse.

The outdoor arena lay blanketed with a thin shimmer of frost that caught the light in thousands of tiny sparkles. Poles had already been set in a neat pattern: a few single crossrails, a line of canter poles, and a small vertical at the far end.

Emma felt her pulse quicken.

"Looks like Coach means business today," Riley murmured.

Cade led Knightfall into the ring with a quiet confidence that made Riley raise an eyebrow at Emma.

"He thinks he already knows the pattern," Riley whispered.

"He is probably just used to this kind of training," Emma whispered back.

But part of her wondered if Riley was partially right.

They mounted up, and the lesson began with warm-up circles at the walk, then the trot. The cold air sharpened everything: the sound of hooves, the rustle of coats, the smell of the earth.

Willow moved willingly underneath Emma, each step steady and responsive. Emma felt the mare's warmth seep into her legs as she eased her hands into the rhythm. It felt grounding. Familiar. Safe.

But every time she circled near Knightfall, she noticed the same odd pause. The smallest moment where he seemed to think before he moved.

He was not lame. Not stiff enough for anyone else to notice. But Emma saw it again. A flicker.

And her worry returned.

Coach Sloane called out, "Let us move into cantering. Establish a forward rhythm. Shoulders back."

Emma asked Willow for the transition, and the mare lifted lightly into the gait. Ember surged into canter with Riley, a little too enthusiastically. Chase hesitated, but Harper coaxed him along gently. Daisy moved slowly but dutifully with Zoey.

Knightfall collected himself, then stepped into the canter under Cade's steady cue.

Again, just a fraction late.

Again, subtle.

Cade did not react. Coach Sloane did not seem to see it.

But Emma noticed.

As they continued cantering, Coach Sloane raised her voice above the rhythmic thudding of hooves. "Today we begin working on your first medal pattern. Focus on approaching fences straight and maintaining pace. Prepare to trot over the first crossrail."

Riley grinned. "Finally."

Emma guided Willow toward the first jump. The mare lifted cleanly, her knees folding neatly as they popped over the crossrail. Emma landed softly, shoulders relaxed.

Harper followed, Chase clearing the jump with cautious effort. Zoey came next, Daisy flicking an ear back but floating over easily.

Then Cade turned Knightfall toward the crossrail.

Knightfall approached steadily, ears forward, stride rhythmic.

Emma exhaled. Maybe everything was fine.

Knightfall lifted.

Then he stopped.

Abruptly.

His front hooves planted firmly in the dirt, sending Cade pitching slightly forward. Cade caught himself quickly, pulling Knightfall back into line with controlled hands.

Riley gasped. Harper froze. Zoey's breath caught.

Emma felt her stomach wrench.

Coach Sloane stepped forward, voice sharp but controlled.

"Cade. Circle and approach again. Give him time to think but keep your leg on."

"Yes, Coach," Cade responded instantly.

He circled Knightfall in a tight loop. The gelding snorted, tossing his head with tension Emma had not seen before. Cade straightened him out, lined him up with the crossrail, and asked again.

Knightfall trotted forward.

And again stopped before the jump.

Not violently. Not dramatically.

Just a hard, sudden refusal.

Cade steadied himself. "He has never done this with me."

Coach Sloane's jaw tightened slightly. "Knightfall is not known for refusals. Something is bothering him. Keep him moving. Let us try one more time."

Emma's pulse raced. Knightfall did not refuse. He did not panic. He was one of the most reliable horses at Saddle Creek. Something was wrong. She could feel it in her bones.

Riley leaned toward Emma, whispering urgently, "He never does that. Never."

Emma swallowed hard. "I know."

Harper bit her lip. "Do you think Cade is doing something wrong?"

Emma hesitated.

Cade's hands were steady. His seat was balanced. His posture correct. His cues clear.

Knightfall was not refusing because of Cade's riding.

He was refusing because something inside him was telling him to stop.

Coach Sloane nodded to Cade. "One more approach. Slow. Controlled. Leg on. Give him confidence."

Cade circled again, his face calm but focused. He guided Knightfall forward, step by step.

Emma leaned forward unconsciously, gripping the reins tighter.

Knightfall approached the jump.

His ears flicked forward.

His head lowered slightly.

And then, at the very last second...

He stopped.

This time Cade stayed perfectly balanced, sitting deep in the saddle without being thrown forward.

Knightfall froze, legs locked, breath quick and shallow.

Coach Sloane stepped forward, her expression turning from firm to thoughtful.

"That is enough for today," she said gently. "Cade, walk him around the ring. Something is bothering him. We do not push a horse through discomfort."

Cade nodded, though Emma could see frustration in his shoulders.

Riley whispered, "Knightfall has never done that in his entire life."

Harper added quietly, "Something must be wrong."

Zoey murmured, "What do we do?"

Emma felt her heart pounding. She looked at Knightfall, who now walked with a slightly uneven rhythm. Still not lame. Still nothing dramatic. But the unease in his body was unmistakable to her.

Coach Sloane addressed the group. "Continue with your pattern practice. We will skip Knightfall for now."

Emma guided Willow forward mechanically. She jumped the next crossrail cleanly, but her stomach twisted with every stride. Her eyes kept drifting toward Cade and Knightfall, who circled the arena slowly.

Knightfall's breathing slowly evened out, but his ears stayed pinned slightly back. His eyes darted in small, nervous movements.

He was not himself. Not even close.

By the end of the lesson, Emma could barely focus. Riley seemed rattled. Harper kept sneaking worried glances. Zoey stayed quiet, her expression tight and pale.

When Coach Sloane dismissed them, Emma dismounted immediately and walked Willow toward the gate.

Cade was already leading Knightfall out, his expression unreadable. When Emma passed him, he muttered under his breath, "I did everything right."

Emma stopped, surprised by the emotion in his voice. "You did. Anyone could see that."

He turned to her, frustration flickering behind his dark eyes. "Then why did he refuse three times?"

Emma hesitated, then spoke carefully. "Sometimes horses refuse because they feel something physically. Not pain that is obvious. Sometimes just... discomfort."

Cade looked at Knightfall, then back at Emma. "He jumped fine yesterday."

Emma swallowed. "He hesitated yesterday too. A little. Not as much. But I noticed."

Cade's eyes widened. "You saw it?"

Emma nodded. "It was small. But yes."

Cade looked at Knightfall again, listening quietly.

It was the first moment he seemed open. Not defensive. Not proud. Just... uncertain.

"We can tell Coach Sloane," Emma offered softly. "Or the barn manager. They will know what to check."

Cade nodded slowly. "Yeah. I think you are right."

It was a small moment. But a real one.

Emma watched him lead Knightfall toward the barn, one hand resting gently on the gelding's neck. Cade was serious. Intense. But he cared. She could see it now.

Riley approached Emma from behind. "So. Knightfall refused. That is new."

Emma nodded, her stomach still knotted. "I know."

"Do you think Cade caused it?"

Emma shook her head. "No. I think Knightfall is trying to tell us something."

Harper joined them, worry etched across her face. "Should we mention it to Coach Sloane?"

"We should," Emma said. "But Cade is already doing that. He knows something is wrong."

Zoey stood a few steps behind them, hugging Daisy's lead rope close to her chest. "This is scary."

Emma nodded gently. "It is. But we will figure it out."

As the four girls walked back toward the barn, frost began melting into glittering droplets that dripped from the fence posts.

A new rider had arrived.

A dependable horse was beginning to falter.

And an unsettling feeling had settled deep inside Emma's chest.

Something was shifting at Saddle Creek.

Something big.

This winter would not be easy.

And Knightfall's refusal was only the beginning.

Chapter Four

By the next day, it felt like the entire barn had heard about Knightfall's refusal.

Emma did not understand how news traveled so fast at Saddle Creek, but somehow it always did. The barn was like a woven net. Tug on one string, and the whole thing shook. By the time Emma arrived for her afternoon ride, whispers drifted through the aisles like cold wind slipping under a door.

"I heard he refused three times."

"Coach Sloane looked upset."

"Maybe the new boy did something wrong."

"No, Knightfall never refuses. Something is wrong with him."

"Do not tell Cade. He looked angry."

Emma felt her chest tighten as she passed a group of younger riders near the feed room. They were gathered in a small circle, whispering loudly enough for her to hear. She wished she could make them stop. It was not fair to Knightfall. It was not fair to Cade either.

Willow whickered softly from her stall as Emma walked in. The mare's warm breath and gentle eyes steadied her, like they always did. Emma stroked her forehead and buried her face in Willow's mane for a moment, inhaling the familiar scent of hay and warm coat.

"Everything feels weird today," Emma whispered.

Willow leaned into her hand. Solid. Calm. Steady.

Emma wished the rest of the barn felt the same.

The sound of boots approaching made her look up. Riley strode in, cheeks pink and expression stormy.

"Okay," Riley said without preamble. "Half the barn thinks Cade caused Knightfall's refusal. The other half thinks Knightfall hates him. And there is a small but very dramatic third group who think Knightfall is cursed."

Emma blinked. "Cursed?"

"Yes," Riley said, tossing her hair in frustration. "Cursed. I heard someone say he probably sensed Cade's 'dark energy' and freaked out."

Emma nearly laughed, but the knot in her stomach kept the smile small.

"It is not funny," Riley added. "This is going to cause drama. I can feel it."

Harper entered the aisle a moment later, clutching Chase's lead rope. "I heard someone say Cade yanked too hard on the reins."

Emma sighed. "He did not yank. He was calm. I watched him."

Zoey trailed behind Harper, Daisy plodding loyally at her side. "People are saying Knightfall is dangerous now."

Emma's chest tightened more. "Knightfall is not dangerous. He was telling us he did not feel right."

Riley crossed her arms. "Do you think he is sick?"

Emma hesitated before answering. "I think something is bothering him physically. Or maybe the weather. Or pressure. Or something small that is turning into something bigger."

Zoey looked down, twisting her fingers nervously. "I do not want anyone to think our horses are unpredictable."

Emma stepped closer, placing a gentle hand on Zoey's arm.

"Knightfall is not unpredictable. He is smart. He is always trying to communicate. He is just... asking for help right now."

Zoey nodded, but worry still clouded her eyes.

Coach Sloane appeared outside the tack room with a clipboard in hand. Her steps were sharp, her jaw tight. Not angry, exactly. More like determined.

"Everyone," she called. "Listen up, please."

The girls stepped forward. Several other riders gathered too, drawn in by the tone of her voice.

"There are rumors going around," Coach Sloane said plainly. "Let me be clear. Knightfall is being evaluated. The vet will visit tomorrow morning. Until then, he will not be ridden."

A hush fell over the aisle.

Coach Sloane continued, "I do not want to hear any more gossip. Cade did nothing wrong. Knightfall is not dangerous. We respect our horses first, and we do not blame riders for something they did not cause."

Riley shot Emma a quick look that said see, I told you this would blow up.

Emma swallowed, relieved and anxious at the same time.

Coach Sloane dismissed the group with a firm nod and walked toward the office.

But the silence she left behind did not last long.

The whispers started again as soon as she was gone, quieter this time but still swirling through the barn like dust in sunlight.

"See, the vet is coming. Something is wrong."

"Maybe Knightfall strained something."

"Maybe Cade pushed him too hard."

Emma clenched her jaw.

Before she could say anything, Cade appeared from the far end of the barn, leading Knightfall by a loose lead rope. His posture was stiff, shoulders tense. Knightfall walked calmly beside him, but the gelding's ears kept flicking backward, as if sensing the tension in Cade's body or the atmosphere around him.

As Cade passed a pair of older riders, they fell silent. One of them stared at him openly. Cade's jaw tightened. His eyes hardened.

Emma stepped forward before she could think about it.

"Hi," she said gently.

Cade paused. "Hi."

She glanced at Knightfall, then back at him. "How is he today?"

"Still stiff," Cade said quietly. "He feels weird when he walks. Not limping. Just... off."

Emma nodded. "I saw that yesterday."

Cade let out a slow breath. "Everyone thinks it is my fault."

"It is not your fault," Emma said firmly. "You rode well."

Cade looked at her for a long moment, as if trying to decide whether to believe her.

Then he nodded.

Harper approached hesitantly. "Knightfall is strong. He will get better."

Cade gave a small, grateful nod, but his expression stayed closed off. He was not angry. He was... guarded. Emma recognized that feeling too well. The feeling of being the new kid, the outsider, the one everyone watched closely and judged quickly.

Before Emma could say anything else, Riley strode toward them with Ember.

"Cade," Riley said bluntly. "If anyone blames you, ignore them. People like to talk."

Cade blinked. "Thanks... I think."

Riley shrugged. "Facts are facts."

Zoey stood silently beside Daisy, watching the exchange with wide eyes.

The tension in the aisle thickened for a moment, then Cade cleared his throat. "I should put Knightfall back. The vet's coming tomorrow, right?"

"Yes," Emma said. "Coach told everyone."

Cade nodded once, then led Knightfall toward his stall.

The moment he turned the corner, the whispers started again.

"He looks upset."

"I would be too."

"Maybe he is hiding something."

Riley scowled. "Some people need to get a hobby."

Emma felt Willow nudge her shoulder gently from the stall. She reached up, resting her forehead against the mare's cheek. Willow's steady warmth grounded her in a way nothing else could.

The lesson that afternoon was quieter than usual. The barn felt heavy, like a storm waiting to break. Coach Sloane kept them busy with flatwork patterns and figure-eights, making sure no one had time to gossip during the ride.

But the tension sat just beneath the surface.

Harper rode carefully, her brow furrowed in concentration. Riley's energy was sharper than usual, her movements clipped and frustrated whenever Ember tossed her head. Zoey looked distracted, her posture stiff, her mind clearly somewhere else.

Emma's thoughts drifted constantly toward Knightfall, even as she asked Willow to lengthen her stride and circle tightly.

After the lesson ended, the girls gathered near the arena gate to cool their horses.

Riley exhaled loudly. "This is going to get worse, I can feel it."

Harper nodded. "People love talking about drama."

Zoey looked down, speaking softly. "I really hope Knightfall is okay."

Emma nodded. "Me too."

But deep down, she felt something cold and uncertain. Knightfall's refusal was not normal. His stiffness was not normal. And the shifting mood in the barn was not normal either.

Change was rippling through Saddle Creek.

People sensed it.

Horses sensed it.

Emma sensed it most of all, though she could not explain why.

As she stroked Willow's neck, watching frost begin to creep into the corners of the arena again, Emma felt a chill settle along her spine.

This winter was going to be harder than any of them expected.

And the rumors were only the beginning.

Chapter Five

The morning of Knightfall's vet check dawned gray and heavy, the kind of morning where the world felt quieter than usual. The fog hung low over the paddocks, softening everything into blurred outlines. Even the horses seemed subdued, their breaths forming clouds that drifted into the still air.

Emma arrived early, hoping the barn would be empty long enough for her to clear her head. But as soon as she stepped inside, she heard hushed voices. She recognized Riley's laugh first, then Harper's gentle tone. She followed the sound to the grooming bays, where Riley was brushing Ember with determined energy.

"She is shedding early," Riley grumbled, flicking away a tuft of winter coat. "It is like she is trying to turn the aisle into a nest."

Harper looked up from Chase, her face warm with a smile. "Maybe she wants to help us decorate for winter."

Zoey stood a few steps away, quietly tying Daisy in her grooming spot. Her shoulders were hunched, her movements slow and careful, her face pale under the aisle lights.

Emma approached Willow's stall and gave her mare a soft hug before walking over to the others. "Morning."

Riley turned briskly toward her. "Did you hear? The vet is coming at nine. Cade got here already. He is hand-walking Knightfall in the small arena."

Emma nodded. "I saw them outside."

"Good," Riley said sharply. "At least he is taking it seriously."

Harper blinked. "Riley, he has been taking it seriously from the start."

Riley shrugged. "Maybe."

Emma leaned against Willow's stall, watching the way Riley brushed Ember with quick, choppy strokes. Something was bothering her friend. Something more than just Knightfall's situation.

"Did something happen?" Emma asked gently.

Riley blew out a sharp breath. "Nothing happened. People are just dramatic. And noisy. And blaming the wrong people."

Zoey stiffened slightly. Emma noticed the subtle shift, the way Zoey's fingers tightened around Daisy's lead rope.

Harper lowered her brush. "Who is blaming the wrong people?"

"Everyone," Riley snapped. "Some riders are blaming Cade. Some are blaming Coach Sloane. Some think Knightfall is dangerous now, which is completely ridiculous. I heard someone say he should be retired."

Zoey's head jerked up. "That is not true."

"I know it is not true," Riley replied, dropping her brush into her grooming box with a loud clatter. "But people like having something to talk about."

Zoey flinched at the sound.

Emma moved closer. "Zoey, are you okay?"

"I am fine," Zoey murmured.

Riley frowned. "You do not look fine."

Zoey's lips tightened. "I said I am fine."

The three girls exchanged uneasy looks. Zoey was usually quiet, but never curt. Never cold.

Emma stepped carefully beside her. "Zoey, you can talk to us if you want."

Zoey shook her head quickly, almost defensively. "It is nothing."

But her voice cracked.

And Emma saw something break just behind Zoey's eyes, something she had not noticed before because it was hidden under all the noise about Knightfall and Cade.

Something deeper.

Before Emma could speak again, the barn door opened and the vet walked in with a rolling medical case.

The moment snapped.

Everyone straightened.

Cade appeared at the vet's side, Knightfall walking slowly beside him. The gelding looked tired, more than usual. His ears twitched but stayed slightly back, and his steps were measured, thoughtful.

Riley tensed. Harper's expression softened. Zoey's hands twisted at her sleeves.

Emma stepped toward the aisle, heart pounding.

Coach Sloane followed the vet, her expression focused and unreadable.

"Let us give them space," she said softly to the riders.

The girls drifted toward the wall, watching quietly as the vet examined Knightfall. Cade held the gelding's lead rope with steady hands, but his jaw was tight, his eyes fixed on the vet's movements. He looked like he had not slept much.

Riley whispered in a low voice, "Do you think it is something serious?"

Harper bit her lip. "I hope not."

Zoey stood stiffly beside them, watching the exam with fear flickering in her eyes.

Emma watched Knightfall lift each leg for the vet, watched the careful palpation of his shoulder, the bent knees, the slow head lowering. She watched Cade's quiet worry and Coach Sloane's controlled breathing.

She felt Willow shift restlessly behind her in the stall, as if feeling Emma's tension.

After several long minutes, the vet stepped back.

"Well?" Cade asked, voice low.

The vet wiped his hands. "It looks like a mild shoulder strain. Nothing severe. Probably from slipping in the paddock with the frost."

Cade exhaled a breath he had clearly been holding. Riley's tense shoulders dropped. Harper smiled faintly.

Zoey whispered, "Thank goodness."

The vet continued, "He needs rest. No jumping for a few weeks. Light riding only. Warm compresses. Careful stretching. He will recover well."

Coach Sloane nodded. "Thank you."

Cade placed a gentle hand on Knightfall's neck. Emma saw relief spread slowly across his face.

But the relief in the riders around her did not dissolve the tension that had begun forming between them.

Not even close.

After the vet left, the barn returned to its usual rhythm, but everything felt... off. The tension was small but sharp, like a thorn under a saddle pad. Tiny. Hidden. But irritating enough to cause discomfort with every step.

The girls led their horses into the outdoor arena for a light flatwork lesson. The air stayed cold, fog lingering in patches along the edges of the ring. Willow walked beside Emma with a steady rhythm, her ears flicking forward and back, noticing everything.

Zoey trailed behind them with Daisy, hardly speaking.

Riley stormed ahead with Ember, frustration simmering at every movement. Harper kept Chase calm, though Chase snorted at the cold and stepped sideways more than usual.

Emma hoped the lesson would help reset the mood.

But Coach Sloane seemed sharper today too, more serious than usual. She lined them up and gave instructions quickly.

"Today is light flatwork. No pressure. Focus on consistency and quiet hands."

Riley muttered, "Tell that to the rumor mill."

Emma shot her a look. "Riley."

"What?" Riley said, shrugging. "I am being honest."

Zoey's face tightened again.

They rode in silence for several minutes. Willow moved beautifully, her steps soft and elastic. Emma tried to breathe with her mare's rhythm, letting the worries slide off her like water.

But the tension between the girls grew like a quiet, invisible storm.

When Coach Sloane called for a canter transition, Ember tossed her head and nearly bumped into Daisy. Zoey yanked Daisy away with a gasp.

"Riley," Zoey said, voice trembling. "Watch where you are going."

"I did watch," Riley snapped. "Ember is just fresh."

"You were too close," Zoey whispered.

"You always think someone is too close," Riley shot back. "Daisy gets nervous if a leaf blows."

Zoey flinched. "That is not fair."

Emma felt the shift. The fracture forming. The thin edge of something sharp.

She rode closer. "Riley, calm down."

Riley pulled Ember into a circle. "I am calm."

"You are not," Harper said quietly.

Riley stopped, glaring at both of them. "Why is it always my fault? Ember does one little thing and everyone jumps down my throat."

Zoey's voice shook. "I never said it was your fault."

"You might as well have," Riley snapped. "You never speak up until it is to complain about someone being too close, or too fast, or too loud."

Zoey's eyes filled with tears. "I do not do that."

"Yes, you do," Riley said harshly. "You do it all the time."

"Riley, stop," Emma said firmly.

Riley ignored her. "Maybe if you were more confident, Daisy would be too."

Zoey gasped. "I am trying."

"Try harder then," Riley said.

Zoey turned her face away, tears slipping down her cheeks as she guided Daisy to the far end of the ring.

Harper looked horrified. "Riley…"

Emma rode up beside Zoey but did not try to speak yet. She knew Zoey needed a moment, needed space. Daisy walked quietly, her steps small and careful as if sensing Zoey's distress.

Coach Sloane called out from the center, her voice cutting through the tension. "Eyes up. Keep your spacing. Riley, maintain your track."

Her tone was firm, but she had not heard the argument itself. Or maybe she chose not to intervene yet.

The lesson continued, but the damage had been done. Every movement felt stiff. Every cue felt forced. The air felt dense with unspoken words.

Zoey stayed at the far rail, avoiding everyone's eyes. Riley fumed silently. Harper kept glancing nervously between them.

Emma felt her chest ache with the weight of it.

This was not like them.

Yes, they argued sometimes. Yes, Riley had a sharp tongue occasionally. But this felt different.

This felt like the first real fracture in their friend group.

After the lesson, Emma walked Willow back to the barn, her thoughts tangled. She wanted to comfort Zoey. She wanted to talk to Riley. She wanted to fix everything.

But she did not know where to start.

Zoey untacked Daisy in silence, her head lowered, her movements shaky. Harper stayed close, helping with silent gestures, sensing Zoey did not want to talk yet.

Riley stormed through her grooming like she was facing the final round of a competition. Every motion was forceful. Every breath sharp.

Emma approached her softly. "Riley?"

"What," Riley said flatly.

Emma paused. "You were too hard on Zoey."

Riley slammed her brush into the grooming box. "I knew you would say that."

"Because it is true," Emma said gently.

Riley turned on her with frustration in her eyes. "She always acts like she is fragile. Like everything scares her. Like she is going to break if someone breathes near her."

"Zoey is trying," Emma said. "You know she gets overwhelmed."

"So?" Riley shot back. "We all get overwhelmed. You do. I do. Harper does. But Zoey acts like it is the end of the world whenever something goes slightly wrong."

Emma took a breath. "You hurt her today. More than you realize."

Riley paused, anger wavering. For a moment she looked exhausted instead of furious.

"She thinks everyone is mad at her," Emma said softly.

Riley's expression flickered with something vulnerable, but she pushed it away. "She should not assume that."

"You should not assume she is being dramatic," Emma replied.

Riley flung her towel over Ember's back. "Why do I always have to be the one who changes?"

Emma blinked. "Riley, that is not what this is about."

Riley's shoulders slumped. "You all treat Zoey like she is a glass ornament. One bump and she shatters. It is not fair."

"Zoey is sensitive," Emma said quietly. "But that does not make her weak."

Riley stared at Emma for a long moment, her chest rising and falling quickly. Then she stepped away.

"I need a break," she muttered.

And she walked out of the barn, boots crunching loudly on the gravel.

Zoey stayed late.

Emma helped her finish with Daisy even though Zoey did not ask. Harper lingered too, offering soft words when the silence grew too heavy.

Zoey spoke only once.

"Riley hates me."

Emma's heart broke a little. "Zoey, she does not."

"She does," Zoey whispered. "I saw it in her eyes."

Emma shook her head. "She was upset. She said things she did not mean."

Zoey wiped her eyes quickly. "It does not matter. People always say things they do not mean. But they still hurt."

"Zoey," Emma said softly, "Riley cares about you."

Zoey looked down. "Does she?"

"Yes," Emma insisted. "Even when she is frustrated."

Zoey sniffed, not convinced.

Harper gently touched Zoey's arm. "Riley reacts without thinking sometimes. But she always regrets it."

Zoey nodded slowly, though Emma could see she did not fully believe it.

They finished putting Daisy away, and Zoey whispered a small thank you before leaving the barn alone, her footsteps quiet and slow.

Harper sighed. "This is getting bad."

Emma nodded, feeling a weight settle inside her. "We need to fix it."

Harper looked toward the door. "Riley is not ready to talk yet."

"I know," Emma said. "But if we do not help them now, this will get worse."

Harper tucked a loose strand of hair behind her ear. "What do we do?"

Emma looked at Willow, who watched her with calm eyes.

"We start by being patient," Emma said. "And by not letting this turn into something bigger."

Harper nodded. "I will talk to Zoey. You talk to Riley?"

Emma nodded, though worry grew in her chest. "Yes."

But as she gathered Willow's brushes and put them neatly back in her tack trunk, she felt it.

A shift.

A fracture.

Tiny now, but painful.

And deep.

The kind that could grow into something much larger if they were not careful.

The barn felt colder as she closed her trunk, the sunlight dimming outside. The fog thickened, blurring the world beyond the aisle doors.

Emma hugged Willow one more time before leaving. The mare pressed her soft nose into Emma's shoulder, breathing warmth into her.

"We will fix this," Emma whispered.

But she did not know how yet.

Only that winter was close now, close enough to feel in the chill of the air and the tension in the barn.

And friendship, like horses, was something fragile that needed careful hands.

Because once a fracture formed, it did not disappear on its own.

It had to be healed.

Slowly.

Patiently.

Together.

Chapter Six

The morning of the schooling show began colder than any day so far that fall. Frost wrapped itself around the fence posts like thin white fingers, and a delicate sheet of ice covered the water troughs in the paddocks. A pale sun struggled to rise through the gray haze that clung low above Saddle Creek.

Emma stood in the barn aisle dressed in her show clothes, hugging Willow's neck for warmth and calm. She pressed her cheek against the mare's soft coat and breathed in the familiar scent of clean shavings and winter grass. Willow flicked her ears forward, as if sensing Emma's nerves.

"I know," Emma whispered. "I am nervous too."

She was not only nervous about the schooling show. The tension between her friends still lingered like a fog that would not lift. Riley had been quiet for two days, barely speaking in lessons. Zoey avoided her entirely and looked crushed every time Riley walked past. Harper stayed stuck in the middle, trying to help both sides but unable to fix anything.

And Cade... Cade had grown quieter since Knightfall's diagnosis. He spoke only when necessary, kept to himself, and worked with

Knightfall gently under Coach Sloane's eye. The vet had cleared the gelding for light riding, but jumping was still out of the question. Cade would not be competing today.

The barn felt strange without him in the show roster.

Strange in a way Emma did not like.

She heard footsteps and turned to see Riley entering the aisle, Ember in tow. Riley was dressed and ready, but her expression was distant, her eyes fixed ahead like she was going into battle.

Harper followed with Chase, her breathing calm but her posture tight. Zoey trailed behind, carrying Daisy's bridle and looking smaller than usual, as if the weight of the conflict rested on her shoulders alone.

Emma watched them all gather near the grooming bays, the four of them lining up without speaking.

Coach Sloane's voice cut through the cold air. "Riders, gather around."

Everyone stepped closer. Emma stood just beside Willow, gently stroking the mare's neck.

"This is your first schooling show of the season," Coach Sloane said. "Remember that today is about learning. There will be mistakes. There will be surprises. What matters is how you handle them."

Her eyes flicked briefly toward Riley, then toward Zoey. Neither girl responded.

Coach continued, "Warm up slowly. Do not rush your horses. Focus on straight lines, consistent pace, and clear communication. The course today is basic but technical. You will need to think ahead."

She looked at Emma. "You start first. Willow is ready."

Emma nodded, her heart thudding.

Riley lifted her chin. Harper inhaled softly. Zoey clutched Daisy's reins so hard her knuckles whitened.

Emma moved toward the mounting block with Willow, trying to shake off the chill in her limbs. As she swung into the saddle, she felt

Willow steady beneath her. The mare's calm presence warmed her from the inside.

"You and me, girl," Emma whispered.

Willow flicked her ears and stepped toward the arena.

The warm-up ring was already crowded. Horses crunched frost beneath their hooves. Riders trotted in wide circles, calling out warnings as they passed. The tension in the air was palpable. Too many riders. Too little space. Too many nerves.

Emma guided Willow along the outside track, letting the mare warm her muscles. Willow's breath puffed into the air in soft white clouds. She moved smoothly at the trot, her steps light and elastic. Emma focused on her breathing, counting her strides, settling her mind.

But around her, chaos hummed beneath the surface.

A girl from Silver Spur cut in front of Riley with barely an inch to spare. Ember tossed her head and snorted loudly.

"Watch it," Riley snapped.

The girl laughed and kept trotting.

Harper frowned, adjusting Chase's reins as she tried to keep him calm. Chase danced sideways when a pony zipped past too quickly, nearly colliding with Daisy.

Zoey tensed instantly, clutching the reins. "Careful," she whispered, her voice cracking with fear.

The pony's rider did not even look back.

Emma clenched her jaw. The warm-up ring always brought out the worst in some riders. No one meant to be dangerous, but nerves made people reckless. And today... today everything felt worse.

Cade stood at the rail, watching silently while Knightfall rested in a nearby paddock. Emma caught his eye briefly. He gave her a faint nod, like he hoped she would do well. Or maybe like he wanted to be out there too.

Emma straightened her shoulders.

She would ride well. For Willow. For herself.

"Emma, you are up next," Coach Sloane called from the gate. "One more canter circle, then come in."

Emma turned Willow and asked for the canter. Willow lifted into the gait smoothly, her body warm and powerful beneath Emma. The mare's energy filled Emma with confidence, the nerves melting away with each stride.

She slowed Willow back to a trot, then walked toward the gate.

"You can do this," Harper whispered as they passed.

Emma smiled. "Thanks."

She entered the arena, letting the quiet settle around her. The schooling show ring felt different from the warm-up. Colder. Larger. Calmer. The course stood neatly set: a simple pattern of crossrails and small verticals, decorated with fall flowers and bright flags.

Emma breathed out, remembering Coach Sloane's words.

Today is about learning.

She picked up a trot and began her course.

Willow moved willingly, responding to each cue with trust. The first crossrail came up quick, but Emma kept her pace steady. Willow lifted neatly over it. The second crossrail approached from a tight turn, but Emma kept her inside leg strong, guiding Willow through.

Then came the small vertical.

Emma exhaled, softened her hands, and Willow soared over it with beautiful form.

As they cantered through the final line, Emma felt something warm and steady rise inside her chest. Confidence. Partnership. Growth.

They crossed the finish and slowed to a walk.

A smattering of claps came from the sideline. Emma spotted Cade watching her ride, his eyes thoughtful. Riley clapped enthusiastically. Harper grinned. Zoey gave a small smile.

Emma patted Willow's neck. "Good girl."

Coach Sloane gave her an approving nod. "Solid ride. Straight approach. Good pace. You are improving."

Emma's chest glowed with pride.

But the moment did not last long.

"Riley, you are next," Coach Sloane called.

And the tension in the air shifted.

Riley strode into the arena with Ember, her posture confident but her expression stormy. Ember snorted, tossing her head restlessly.

Harper leaned toward Emma. "I hope Riley calms down. Ember feels everything."

Emma nodded. "She will. She knows how important this is."

Zoey stood behind them, clutching Daisy's reins with tense fingers. She did not say anything.

Riley trotted Ember forward and began her course.

At first, things went well. Ember cleared the first crossrail easily. She landed with a strong, energetic stride. Riley steadied her going into the second fence, keeping a good rhythm.

But then, in the middle of the course, everything began to unravel.

As Riley approached the vertical, a loud noise echoed from the parking lot. A trailer door slammed. Ember jolted, throwing her head high.

Riley tried to steady her, but Ember surged forward faster than planned.

She jumped the vertical too early, launching higher than needed. Riley barely stayed centered. Ember landed fast, almost losing her balance.

Emma's heart leapt. "Come on, Riley," she whispered.

Riley tried to regain control, but Ember tossed her head, agitated by the cold and the crowd.

The final fence approached too quickly.

Riley circled, but the circle was messy and rushed. Ember nearly collided with the rail before Riley corrected her.

When she finally finished, Coach Sloane sighed softly. "Rushed. Tense. But you recovered. We will work on rhythm later."

Riley looked furious, not at Ember, but at herself.

She stormed out of the ring.

Harper and Emma exchanged anxious glances.

Zoey stepped aside nervously as Riley passed, but Riley did not even look at her.

Harper rode next and did well. Chase hesitated once, but Harper guided him kindly, and they finished with a neat round. Emma cheered for her, and Harper smiled shyly.

Then it was Zoey's turn.

Zoey mounted Daisy with trembling hands.

Emma walked to the gate. "Zoey. You can do this."

Zoey nodded, but the fear in her eyes was stark.

She rode into the arena, the smallest rider on the smallest horse, looking swallowed by the cold and the space.

Her trot was steady at first.

Then Daisy spooked at a bright blue flower pot beside the first jump. Zoey gasped, yanking the reins.

"Zoey, steady your hands," Coach Sloane called.

Zoey tried, but the panic had already crept in.

Daisy rushed forward, throwing off the timing. When Zoey approached the first crossrail, she took it too slow. Daisy stumbled on landing.

Zoey's face crumpled with fear.

She circled, but the circle grew too wide, carrying her close to the arena rail. Daisy flicked her ears nervously.

When Zoey finally finished the messy course, she looked close to tears.

Coach Sloane kept her voice gentle. "Good effort. We will work on confidence exercises this week."

Zoey nodded silently and rode out of the ring.

Emma met her at the gate. "Zoey, hey, you finished. That was brave."

Zoey looked away. "It was terrible."

"No, it was brave," Emma insisted. "That matters."

Zoey said nothing. She mounted down and hurried toward the barn.

Riley muttered under her breath, "She only thinks it was terrible because I upset her."

Emma whipped her head around. "Riley. Stop. This is not the time."

Riley clenched her jaw. "I did nothing wrong."

Emma took a breath. "You hurt her."

"No," Riley said coldly. "She chose to get upset."

Emma stared at her. "That is not fair."

Riley glared back. "Life is not fair."

Harper flinched at the edge in her voice. Cade, standing nearby, looked between them silently.

Emma felt something snap inside her.

This show day was tearing everyone apart.

And the worst part was, winter had not even begun.

The tensions followed the girls into the barn.

Zoey disappeared into Daisy's stall, closing the door behind her. Harper stood helplessly nearby.

Riley brushed Ember aggressively, muttering under her breath.

Emma unbridled Willow and stroked her mane, trying to calm the storm in her chest.

Tears pricked her eyes.

This was not what Saddle Creek was supposed to feel like.

This was not how friendship was supposed to feel.

Harper walked up quietly. "We have to fix this."

Emma nodded, swallowing. "I know."

"But how?" Harper asked.

Emma looked toward Zoey's stall, then toward Riley brushing Ember with angry, clipped motions.

"I do not know," Emma whispered. "But we will."

She hoped.

She really hoped.

Because winter was coming fast, the barn shrinking into smaller, colder spaces as the season deepened.

And fractures in friendships, like fractures in horses, only got worse when pressure built.

Emma stroked Willow once more and exhaled a shaky breath.

"We will fix it," she whispered into Willow's mane.

But she had no idea how.

And deep inside, she feared the storm gathering between her friends was about to break.

Chapter Seven

The next weekend arrived with an icy wind that swept across Saddle Creek like a warning. Emma felt it the moment she stepped out of her mother's car, a sharp gust that tugged at her jacket and scattered brittle leaves along the driveway. It whistled between the barn and the indoor arena, carrying with it the first true bite of the coming winter.

Willow whinnied when she saw Emma, her soft voice echoing through the chilly aisle. Emma hurried to her, pressing her cheek into the mare's warm neck. Willow's breath misted the air, comforting despite the cold.

"Good morning, girl," Emma whispered. "Today is going to be tough. But we can handle tough."

The warm-up session for the medal qualifiers was scheduled for midday, but the barn was already buzzing with nerves. Riders hurried past in show pants and winter jackets. Horses clattered on the concrete aisle as they were led toward the indoor arena. And everywhere Emma turned, she saw tension stretched thin like wire.

Riley was brushing Ember hard enough to fluff up the mare's coat. Harper was quietly adjusting Chase's saddle, her eyes darting nervously toward the indoor. Zoey stayed glued to Daisy's side, silent, pale, and careful like every noise might shatter her.

Cade leaned against Knightfall's stall door, watching the others warm up. The gelding was still on light work only, so Cade would not be riding today either. Knightfall's strain was improving, but he needed another week of rest. Cade's posture was stiff, his jaw tight, as if sitting out today cut deeper than he wanted anyone to know.

Emma felt it too. Something in the air vibrated with unease. The last schooling show had left burns on every friendship thread between them, and those threads were fraying more each day.

"Emma, you ready?" Riley asked, but her voice was sharper than curious.

"Almost," Emma replied, brushing Willow's mane into neat, careful lines.

Harper stepped closer. "Have you seen the warm-up ring? There are so many riders. And Silver Spur is here again."

Zoey trembled slightly at the name. "They ride so fast."

"Too fast," Riley muttered. "Too rude."

Emma tried to steady her own breathing. Crowded warm-up rings had never been her favorite, but since the last show, they felt even more intimidating.

Coach Sloane stepped into the aisle, clipboard in hand, expression stern but steady. "Riders," she called, "ten minutes until the warm-up session. Get your horses ready and meet at the indoor entrance."

Emma gave Willow a final pat. "We got this," she whispered. The mare flicked her ears as if agreeing.

The friends gathered at the arena entrance, each gripping reins tighter than usual. Cade stood behind them, leaning on the railing. His eyes briefly met Emma's. He gave the smallest nod, an unspoken stay safe.

Emma nodded back.

Coach Sloane opened the gate. "Enter in pairs. Keep right. Walk only until we settle the traffic."

The moment Emma stepped inside, the noise swallowed her. Horses snorted. Riders shouted "Inside!" or "Heads up!" The sound of hooves pelting the footing rang through the cavernous space. Warm breath drifted in clouds, mixing with dust in the cold light filtering through the high windows.

Silver Spur riders zipped around the edges at a strong trot, ignoring the rule to walk first. One almost clipped Harper's stirrup, forcing Chase sideways.

"Hey!" Harper gasped.

The other rider barely glanced back.

Emma's stomach clenched.

She led Willow to the far end, away from the chaos, and mounted up. Riley swung onto Ember with too much force, her frustration flaring. Zoey climbed onto Daisy shakily. Harper mounted last, careful and steady.

Coach Sloane stood in the middle, trying to direct the flow like a traffic officer in a storm.

"Walk on the track. Trot only if there is space. Inside track for canter. Everyone pay attention to where you are going."

But many riders ignored her.

Especially those from Silver Spur.

One trotted straight across Emma's line, cutting her off so abruptly that Willow snorted and tossed her head.

Emma gritted her teeth. "Seriously?" she muttered.

Riley's voice rang across the ring. "Unbelievable."

Harper looked tense. "Please be careful," she whispered to Chase.

Zoey clung to Daisy's mane. "I do not like this."

Emma moved nearer. "You are okay. Just stay near the rail for now."

Zoey nodded but did not look convinced.

Then Cade's voice echoed from the rail. "Emma. Stay aware of your left."

She looked sharply left just in time to see a chestnut pony

barreling toward her. She tugged Willow aside, avoiding a collision by inches. Her heart jolted into her throat.

"Thank you," Emma called toward Cade.

He nodded once but said nothing more.

Coach Sloane's voice grew louder, more urgent. "Silver Spur riders, please slow down. You are creating unsafe conditions."

A girl from Silver Spur tossed her hair, pretending not to hear.

Riley muttered, "Or they just do not care."

Emma tried to block everything out and focus on Willow. The mare's ears flicked anxiously at the noise, but she trusted Emma's hands and moved into a soft walk. Emma tried to stay calm for both of them.

Coach Sloane finally signaled. "All Saddle Creek riders, trot now. Single file until you have space."

Emma squeezed Willow into a trot. Harper followed, then Zoey, then Riley. The ring swarmed with bodies. Horses brushed stirrups. Riders squeaked by each other too close.

The tension in the air thickened, pressing against Emma's skin.

Warm-up rings were supposed to be chaotic, but this was something else. This was dangerous.

Emma heard Cade curse softly under his breath as another rider swerved recklessly across the ring.

Then the chaos peaked.

A Silver Spur rider attempted to canter through the inside track without warning. Her horse surged forward, spooking a small bay pony that veered sharply toward Daisy.

Zoey screamed.

Daisy skidded sideways. Zoey clung on, her body thrown off balance.

Emma reacted instantly. "Zoey, sit back!"

Zoey tried, but her panic froze her.

Emma urged Willow through the traffic, weaving between cantering horses and frantic riders. Harper tried to help but Chase balked at the commotion.

Riley shouted at the Silver Spur rider, "Watch where you are going!"

The rider smirked and continued.

Zoey's breath hitched violently. Daisy danced, hindquarters swinging dangerously close to another horse.

Emma reached them in seconds.

"Zoey, breathe," she instructed. "Look at me. Not at Daisy."

Zoey finally tore her gaze from Daisy's frantic feet and looked at Emma, tears breaking through.

"Emma," she cried. "I cannot. I cannot. I will fall."

"You will not," Emma said firmly. "I am right here."

Emma guided Willow up beside Daisy's shoulder, careful and steady. Willow, calm under pressure, steadied Daisy by her presence alone. Daisy exhaled shakily, her trembling easing at the sight of Willow.

Zoey gulped for air.

"You are okay," Emma said softly, leaning closer. "Breathe with me."

Zoey matched her breath shakily. Daisy slowed.

Coach Sloane pushed through the chaos toward them. "Everyone halt. Now."

Every horse skidded into a stop. Riders looked around uneasily.

Coach Sloane pointed sharply at the Silver Spur girl who caused the near-collision. "You. Out. Now. You are done for this warm-up session."

The girl scoffed. "What? For what?"

"For dangerous riding," Coach Sloane said, her tone freezing. "And for endangering others."

The Silver Spur rider rolled her eyes dramatically but walked out of the ring, her trainer shooting Coach Sloane a glare.

The moment she left, tension eased slightly, like a storm cloud parting just enough to let in a streak of sunlight.

Coach Sloane looked around. "Take a few minutes to breathe."

She moved to Zoey. "Zoey, you did well to stay on. Daisy too."

Zoey nodded shakily.

Emma stroked Willow's neck. "Good girl."

The warm-up resumed in a calmer, slower pace at Coach Sloane's insistence. She divided the ring, sending half the riders to walk in a separate lane while the others practiced smooth trots.

Emma stayed close to Zoey and Harper, keeping them in her peripheral vision.

But Riley...

Riley simmered.

She kept glancing toward the Silver Spur riders still in the ring, her expression darkening.

Emma guided Willow next to her. "Riley. Let it go."

Riley shot her a sharp look. "They almost made Zoey fall. And they have been reckless all morning. No one does anything."

"Coach Sloane did," Emma reminded.

"Too late," Riley snapped. "Zoey could have been hurt."

Emma sighed. "Riley, do not start again."

"Start what?" Riley said, her voice rising. "Telling the truth?"

"Riley," Harper whispered nervously. "Please calm down."

"I am calm," Riley said sharply. "But it is ridiculous. Zoey gets scared of everything, and then chaos happens. It is exhausting."

Zoey stiffened.

Emma's heart twisted. "Riley... not now."

Zoey's voice trembled. "Sorry."

Riley looked at her. "There you go again. You say sorry for something that is not even your fault. That is what I mean."

Zoey's face crumpled. "I am just trying."

"Trying is not enough when people can get hurt," Riley said.

Emma's voice sharpened. "Stop."

Riley whipped her head toward Emma. "Stop what? Saying what everyone is thinking?"

"Not everyone," Harper said quietly.

Riley exhaled, frustrated and furious. "Whatever."

Emma felt the fracture widening again, deeper than before.

The warm-up continued, but the atmosphere remained tense. Every trot circle felt heavy. Every canter transition felt unstable. The air seemed charged and brittle.

When the warm-up ended, Coach Sloane called all Saddle Creek riders to the corner.

"That was chaotic," she said bluntly. "But you held it together better than most."

Her eyes flicked knowingly toward Emma and Zoey. "Some of you handled danger with maturity."

Then she looked at Riley. "Some of you let emotion take over."

Riley bristled. "I was just—"

"This is not a discussion," Coach Sloane said firmly.

Riley looked away, jaw clenched.

Emma's chest hurt.

Coach continued, "You have ten minutes before the medal qualifier rounds begin. Use them wisely. Focus. Breathe. Do not let the warm-up rattle you."

Then she released them.

The moment the girls stepped out of the ring, Zoey rushed ahead, disappearing into the barn aisle. Harper followed, calling gently after her.

Emma turned to Riley. "You cannot keep doing this."

Riley's eyes flashed. "Doing what?"

"Attacking Zoey every time she struggles."

"I am not attacking her," Riley snapped. "I am telling the truth. She panics over everything."

Emma felt something break. "That does not mean you can hurt her."

Riley stared at her.

Then Cade approached quietly. "Riley. Emma is right."

Riley glared at him. "You have been here five minutes. Stay out of it."

Cade did not flinch. "I know panic when I see it. And I know when someone is scared. Zoey was scared. Not dramatic. Scared."

Riley opened her mouth, ready to argue.

Then she closed it.

Cade looked at Emma. "Good job helping her."

Emma nodded, surprised by the warmth in his voice.

Riley turned away and stormed toward Ember's stall.

Emma stood frozen for a moment, her chest tight with worry and hurt.

Then she walked toward Willow's stall, breathing slowly through the pain in her ribcage. Willow greeted her with a soft nicker, nudging her arm gently.

Emma leaned into the mare, letting her body soften.

"Things are getting worse," Emma whispered into Willow's mane. "I do not know how to fix it."

Willow breathed softly against her shoulder.

Outside, the wind howled along the arena walls.

Inside, Emma felt the storm building around her friendships.

And she knew something had to break before anything could heal.

The warm-up had revealed the cracks.

The medal qualifier itself would widen them.

She could feel it.

Like the cold wind crawling under her skin.

Like winter closing in.

And she was not sure any of them were ready.

Chapter Eight

The warm-up ring chaos left something heavy in the air at Saddle Creek, something sharp and unsettled that clung to every wall of the indoor arena. Even after the riders had left to take their ten-minute break before the medal qualifier, the atmosphere remained thick with tension.

Emma felt that tension in her chest as she stood beside Willow's stall, brushing the mare's neck with slow, steady strokes. Willow leaned into her touch, warm and grounding. But Emma's hands shook slightly, and she could not stop them.

She replayed the near-accident in the warm-up ring again and again. Zoey's white-knuckled grip on Daisy. Riley's sharp voice. The Silver Spur rider slicing through the traffic. Cade's warning. Coach Sloane's anger. The almost-collision that could have sent Zoey crashing into the dirt.

Even now, the memory made Emma's stomach twist.

"Emma," Harper said softly from the next stall, brushing Chase's forelock. "Are you alright?"

Emma nodded slowly. "I think so."

"You helped Zoey," Harper said. "You kept her from falling."

"Willow helped her," Emma corrected. "She followed Willow's calm."

Harper smiled faintly. "You and Willow are a good team."

Emma wished she could feel as confident as Harper sounded.

Zoey sat on an overturned bucket farther down the aisle, still in her saddle. She stared at Daisy's hooves, stroking the pony's neck with small, shaky movements. Daisy stood quietly beside her, as if she understood Zoey needed stillness.

Riley remained near Ember, brushing the mare's coat with stiff, tight motions. Her jaw was clenched. Her eyes darted toward Zoey occasionally, but she never stepped closer.

Emma exhaled shakily. She wanted to fix things between her friends. She wanted to pull them all together and make the tension disappear. But she felt helpless.

"Five minutes," Coach Sloane called from the arena door. "Course walk is done. First rider please get ready."

Emma's heart jumped. She checked Willow's girth again, even though she had already checked it twice. She smoothed her gloves. She tightened her helmet strap.

Harper approached shyly. "You will do great."

"Thank you," Emma whispered.

Riley walked over, still tense. "Emma, do not worry about earlier. Ride your course. Focus on that."

Emma hesitated. "Riley..."

"What?" Riley said defensively.

Emma swallowed. "Please talk to Zoey later. She is hurting."

Riley's eyes flicked away. "She always is."

Emma's chest tightened. "Riley. Please."

Riley did not answer.

Coach Sloane appeared in the doorway. "Emma. Gate in."

Emma stiffened, breath quickening. She hugged Willow's neck one more time. "Okay, girl. Let us try our best."

She led Willow into the arena.

. . .

The medal qualifier arena felt colder than the warm-up ring. The jumps stood neatly arranged, each decorated with autumn flowers. The small verticals cast long shadows across the sand. The course map flashed vividly in Emma's mind: a figure-eight pattern, two cross-rails, a short diagonal line, a rollback to a vertical, and a final long approach.

Willow's hooves thumped softly against the footing as Emma mounted. The mare snorted, warm breath rising into the chilly air.

Emma breathed deeply, allowing Willow's steadiness to flow into her.

"You got this, Emma," Coach Sloane said from the gate.

Emma nodded and walked Willow toward the first line of jumps. She felt every muscle in her body shifting from nervous to focused, from uncertain to ready.

She squeezed her legs gently. Willow stepped into a trot, ears forward, eager.

Emma approached the first crossrail with calm precision. Willow lifted neatly, landing with rhythmic steps.

The second fence came faster. Emma kept her hands soft. Willow flowed over it like water.

Then came the diagonal line. A short stride. A slight bend.

Willow soared over the small vertical, landing with perfect balance.

Emma's heart fluttered with something warm and bright.

Confidence.

She approached the rollback turn, gathering Willow's stride. The mare's hindquarters powered beneath her. They turned cleanly, the jump rising ahead of them—

And they cleared it.

Emma's grin spread across her face. The final long approach lay ahead. She breathed, counted her rhythm, and let Willow carry her.

The mare jumped beautifully, arching her neck in a perfect bascule.

They landed smoothly.

Emma heard clapping from the sideline. Harper. Cade. Even Riley. Zoey too, offering a small but genuine smile.

Emma patted Willow's neck, heart glowing.

"You did amazing," she whispered.

Coach Sloane smiled at her as she exited. "Clean, controlled, confident. Well done."

Emma's spirit soared.

It was the first good thing that had happened all day.

Harper rode next.

Chase tripped once during the diagonal line, but Harper corrected him gently and finished strong. Coach Sloane praised her softness and composure.

Zoey rode Daisy after that. Emma held her breath the entire time. Zoey's eyes were wide. Her hands trembled. But Daisy, sweet and loyal, carried her carefully through every fence.

Zoey's final jump was a little crooked, but she stayed on. She finished without tears. When she left the ring, Harper hugged her. Emma squeezed her hand.

Zoey whispered, "I did it."

Emma smiled. "You did."

Riley rode last.

Emma prayed she would have a good round. That something would crack open in her chest and let the anger out. That she would remember what it felt like to smile.

But Ember was wound up from the warm-up chaos. She charged forward on the first approach. Riley tried to steady her but overcorrected. Ember chipped in at the first crossrail, taking off too close. Riley lurched but held her seat.

The second crossrail was crooked. Ember jumped sideways. Riley cursed under her breath.

On the diagonal line, Ember rushed. Riley tried to circle, but another rider walked too close to the rail, blocking her path. Riley's face burned with frustration as Ember tossed her head violently.

The rollback started okay. Riley regained some control. Ember rounded the turn sharply. But the final long approach…

It fell apart.

Ember built speed too fast. Riley half-halted too strongly.

Ember threw her head high and stopped.

A refusal.

Riley's entire body tensed in shock and humiliation.

Coach Sloane said nothing for several long seconds.

Then, calmly, "Circle. Try again."

Riley's cheeks were red with a mix of anger and embarrassment as she circled Ember.

She approached again.

Ember refused again.

Riley's breath hitched audibly.

The entire arena fell silent.

Emma's chest twisted.

Harper held her hands to her mouth.

Zoey looked devastated.

Cade stared at the jump with concern.

Coach Sloane stepped forward. "That is enough. Walk her out."

Riley dismounted the moment she left the arena. She did not meet anyone's eyes. She held Ember's reins like they were the only thing keeping her upright.

Emma walked toward her, but Riley said sharply, "Do not."

Emma froze.

Riley breathed hard, her voice trembling with anger or shame. "Do not come over here. Do not say anything."

Emma stepped back slowly.

Riley led Ember away in silence.

The fracture between them widened.

· · ·

Fifteen minutes later, while Emma was cleaning Willow's bridle, chaos erupted again.

A scream echoed across the barn.

Emma's heart jumped into her throat. She spun around, nearly dropping the bridle. "What was that?"

Harper ran from the aisle entrance. "Emma, come quickly. Something happened in the indoor."

Emma sprinted after her, fear attacking every nerve in her body. When she reached the doorway, she froze.

The first vertical on the course was higher.

Higher than it had been during the class.

Too high.

Riley stood beside the raised jump, hands shaking, her face white and furious. Her breath came in short bursts. Something close to horror sat in her eyes.

Cade was at her side, eyes wide.

Coach Sloane hurried in from the opposite end of the arena, expression thunderous.

"What happened?" she demanded.

Riley's voice shook. "Emma. Someone changed the jump height. After my refusal. Someone raised it."

Emma's breath vanished.

The vertical was at least six inches taller than it had been during the class. Too tall for the level. Too tall for Ember's approach. Too tall for a young rider who had just had the worst warm-up and worst show of the season.

Emma felt sick.

Harper whispered, "Who would do that?"

Zoey trembled beside her. "Why would someone change the jump? Who would even touch it?"

Cade stepped forward. "Riley came in to practice a simple approach. She saw it immediately. It was higher."

Coach Sloane knelt to check the pins. Her voice dropped to a dangerous quiet. "Someone moved these."

Emma felt a chill crawl down her spine.

Riley's voice cracked. "Someone wanted me to fall."

"No," Emma said immediately, stepping forward. "No one would do that."

Riley's eyes filled with tears she refused to let fall. "Someone did. Someone raised the jump."

Cade's jaw tightened. "This was not an accident."

Harper's voice trembled, "But who... Why..."

Zoey's eyes filled with fear. "Someone could have been hurt."

Emma stared at the raised jump and felt her blood run cold.

Someone had altered the course.

And the chaos that followed was only beginning.

* * *

The arena felt colder than before, as if the temperature had dropped the moment Riley said the words out loud. Emma stared at the raised jump, every detail imprinting itself sharply into her mind: the extra holes up the standard, the metal pins pushed in halfway, the pole resting at a height totally wrong for their level.

It did not look like an accident.

It looked deliberate.

Coach Sloane stood slowly, her expression tight but controlled, the way she always looked when she was thinking five steps ahead. She brushed specks of footing off her gloves and faced the group.

"No one touches a course between rounds except me or the show crew," she said quietly.

Emma felt a shiver run through her.

Zoey whispered, "But... who would do this?"

No one answered.

Around them, the arena lights flickered slightly as a cloud drifted across the sun outside. The shadow deepened the eerie feeling that hung in the space.

Cade knelt near the jump, checking the pins the way the vet had checked Knightfall's shoulder days before. His jaw tightened.

"These were pulled and replaced," he said. "Not all the way. Someone was in a hurry."

Riley swallowed, her voice trembling. "Someone tried to make me jump higher on purpose."

Emma stepped toward her. "Riley... we do not know that."

Riley's eyes snapped to her. "Then who else was it meant for? Someone was messing with the course. Someone wanted someone to get hurt."

Harper shook her head. "That does not make sense. Why would anyone want to cause that?"

Riley let out a sharp, humorless laugh. "Have you seen this barn lately? People are angry. People are jealous. People are stressed. It could be anyone."

Emma flinched. "Riley..."

Cade walked toward them, wiping sand from his gloves. "Let us not jump to conclusions."

Riley turned sharply. "You think this has nothing to do with me?"

Cade met her eyes, steady and unbothered by her anger. "I think panic makes people assume the worst. We need facts before blame."

Riley scoffed and looked away.

Coach Sloane's voice cut through the tension. "Everyone, out of the ring. Now."

Her tone left no room for argument.

The riders filed out quietly, even those from Silver Spur who had returned to the rail after the warm-up. They whispered among themselves as they passed, wide-eyed and uneasy. Word was spreading already. Saddle Creek's riders brought something dangerous into the arena. Someone raised a jump. Someone could have been hurt.

Emma hated how quickly rumors could start.

She felt her chest tighten as she watched Riley storm toward the barn, Ember's reins clutched tightly in her hand. Harper followed at a distance, unsure whether to comfort or give space. Zoey drifted behind them, looking small and fragile.

Emma remained beside the arena gate with Cade.

He was staring at the jump with an expression she could not read.

"Do you think someone did it on purpose?" Emma whispered.

Cade did not look at her. "Someone had to do it."

"That does not mean they meant harm."

"No," Cade said quietly. "But it does not mean they did not."

Emma swallowed. The cold settled deeper into her bones.

"Who would do something like that?" she whispered.

Cade's jaw flexed. "Someone who is angry. Or reckless. Or jealous. Or someone who thought they were being funny."

Emma shook her head. "That is not funny."

Cade met her eyes finally. "I know."

Emma stepped away, her thoughts spinning.

She could feel it. The barn had been shifting for days, like something was cracking beneath the surface. Tensions rising. Friendships shaking. Trust fraying.

Someone had finally acted on that fracture.

Back in the barn, the air felt thick. Horses rustled in their stalls nervously. Riders whispered in tense, confused voices.

Emma passed a pair of younger girls who were brushing a pony.

"Did you hear?" one whispered. "Riley said someone tried to sabotage her."

"That is awful," the other replied. "Do you think someone did?"

Emma clenched her jaw.

Rumors were already blooming like weeds.

She hurried to Willow's stall, wanting to anchor herself again. Willow lowered her head, snorting softly in greeting. Emma pressed her hand against the mare's warm forehead.

"We will get through this," Emma whispered, though she was not sure how.

Harper approached carefully. "Riley is in the tack room. She is really upset."

"I know," Emma said.

Zoey stood beside Harper, her eyes still rimmed with fear. "Why would anyone change the jump? What if Riley had tried it? What if Ember had jumped it too high and... and..."

Her voice trembled.

Emma placed a hand on her shoulder. "Zoey, breathe. It is over."

Zoey shook her head. "No it is not. Something bad is happening. People are angry. People are upset. And now this."

Harper looked down. "We should talk to Coach Sloane."

Emma nodded. "We will."

They walked together down the aisle toward the tack room.

Inside, Riley sat on a wooden bench, Ember's reins dangling loosely from her hand. Her expression was hard, her eyes dark and stormy. But Emma saw something else in them too.

Fear.

Riley lifted her eyes sharply as Emma entered. "Do not tell me to calm down."

Emma paused, keeping her voice soft. "I was not going to. I came to check on you."

Riley let out a long, shaky exhale, her voice breaking. "Emma... someone raised the jump. Someone wanted me to get hurt."

Emma felt her heart twist. "Riley... maybe it was not about you specifically."

Riley scoffed. "Then who was it about? You? Harper? Zoey? Cade? Who?"

Emma chose her words carefully. "We do not know. We cannot assume."

"What if it was someone from Silver Spur?" Riley asked.

Harper said gently, "Their riders left the warm-up ring early. They would not have been near the course."

"What if it was someone here then?" Riley shot back.

Zoey flinched.

Harper hesitated. "That does not make sense."

Riley stood abruptly. "Everything makes sense when people are jealous."

Emma stared. "Jealous of what?"

"Jealous that I ride confidently. Jealous that Ember is talented. Jealous that I usually score well. Jealous that I am not falling apart like Zoey does."

Zoey's breath caught.

Emma stepped forward. "Riley, stop."

"No," Riley said fiercely. "I am done pretending."

Zoey whispered, "Please do not say that."

Riley turned toward her, the frustration finally cracking open. "Zoey, you get scared of everything. Everything. And everyone is always protecting you. Everyone is always gentle with you. And when I am not gentle, I become the villain."

Zoey's eyes filled instantly. "I am trying..."

"I am trying too," Riley said. "But no one sees that."

Emma stepped between them. "Riley, that is not fair."

"Life is not fair," Riley repeated, her voice cold and tired.

Harper swallowed hard. "We are supposed to support each other. We are a team."

Riley shook her head. "No. We used to be a team. Now we are just pretending."

Zoey looked down, tears falling freely. "I never wanted any of this."

Riley sighed, rubbing her forehead. "Neither did I."

Emma felt helpless. The fracture in their group was widening, cracking straight through the center of them.

And then Cade entered the tack room.

He took in the scene quickly: Riley red-eyed and furious, Zoey trembling and tearful, Harper frozen with worry, and Emma caught in the middle with pain in her chest.

Cade spoke gently but firmly. "Coach Sloane wants to see all of you."

Riley stiffened. "Are we in trouble?"

"No," Cade said. "She just needs to talk to you."

Harper looked at Emma nervously. "Do we go now?"

Emma took a slow breath. "We go."

Riley hesitated, then followed.

Zoey wiped her eyes, but tears continued dripping down her cheeks.

Emma walked beside her. "Zoey... I am here."

Zoey nodded weakly.

As they stepped into the aisle, Emma glanced toward Willow's stall. The mare watched with soft, concerned eyes, sensing the tension even from far away.

Emma wished she could stay with Willow.

But this conversation had to happen.

For all of them.

Coach Sloane waited in the arena near the raised jump. She stood with her arms crossed, posture straight but not angry. Not yet.

When the girls approached, she gestured for them to gather.

Cade stepped back to lean against the rail but stayed close enough to listen.

Coach Sloane looked from one girl to the next. "I will make this simple. Someone altered a jump on the course. We do not know why. But we will find out."

Zoey trembled. Riley's jaw clenched. Harper's hands twisted in her coat sleeves.

Coach continued. "But that is not why I asked you here."

Emma blinked. "It is not?"

"No," Coach said. "I want to talk about all of you."

A hush fell across the group.

Coach Sloane looked at Riley. "You are riding with anger. That is dangerous."

Riley lowered her gaze.

She looked at Zoey. "You are riding with fear. That is also dangerous."

Zoey's chin trembled.

She looked at Harper. "You are riding with tension that is not yours. That will exhaust you."

Harper nodded silently.

Then Coach faced Emma. "You are carrying all of their emotions."

Emma froze.

Her breath hitched.

Coach softened her voice. "Emma. That is not your job."

Emma swallowed hard, unable to speak.

Coach stepped back slightly, addressing the entire group. "This is what happens when pressure builds and friends stop trusting themselves and each other. Mistakes happen. Tempers flare. And someone gets hurt."

Her gaze flicked toward the altered jump.

Riley looked away.

Zoey burst into quiet tears.

Harper reached for her hand.

Emma exhaled shakily.

Coach continued, "What happened in the warm-up ring today nearly caused a serious accident. And what happened here afterward could have caused an even worse one."

Silence stretched, cold and heavy.

Riley whispered, "Coach... do you think someone did it on purpose?"

Coach held Riley's gaze for a long moment.

Finally she said, "I think someone acted without thinking. Without consideration. Without understanding the consequences."

Zoey's breath caught. "So it was someone here."

Coach did not confirm or deny. She simply said, "We will handle it. But your job is not to find blame. Your job is to ride. To grow. And to support each other."

Emma felt tears prick her eyes.

Coach added, "This winter will test all of you. The indoor arena is small. The cold makes horses tense. Tempers shorten. Confidence shakes. You need to be stronger together, or you will break apart completely."

Her words settled like frost.

Riley looked visibly shaken.

Zoey wiped her face again.

Harper nodded earnestly.

Emma felt Willow's warm breath press into her memory.

Coach finished softly, "Fix this. Before it gets worse."

She walked away, leaving them in front of the raised jump.

The silence that followed was sharp.

Riley finally whispered, "I did not touch the jump."

Zoey's voice was tiny. "None of us would."

Harper said, "We know."

Emma looked at each of them, her voice quiet but steady. "Then we do what Coach said. We stop fighting. We stop blaming. And we fix this."

Her eyes met Riley's.

Then Zoey's.

Then Harper's.

Each girl nodded slowly, unsure, scared, but willing.

Cade spoke from the rail, surprising them. "For what it is worth, you are stronger together than apart."

Riley shot him a tired glare. "You barely know us."

Cade shrugged. "I know horses. And horses act differently when the herd is stressed."

Emma blinked at him.

He added, "You are a herd. Even if you forget that sometimes."

Harper smiled faintly.

Zoey let out a tiny breath.

Riley rolled her eyes but did not argue.

They walked toward the aisle together. Not healed. Not fixed.

But closer.

Emma paused at the arena exit and turned back once more to the raised jump.

The altered poles gleamed coldly in the pale winter sunlight.

Someone had done this.

Someone inside Saddle Creek.

The thought chilled Emma deeper than the wind blowing through the barn corridor.

She whispered to herself, "This is not over."

And she knew, with certainty, that she was right.

Chapter Nine

The morning after the jump incident felt strangely quiet at Saddle Creek, the kind of quiet that made Emma's skin prickle. Something was different. It was not the weather, though the sharp cold had crept deeper into the soil overnight. It was not the horses, though they moved more tensely than usual, their breaths clouding the air with quick puffs. It was not even the riders, though none of them spoke above a whisper.

It was everything.

The entire barn felt like it was holding its breath.

Emma arrived earlier than usual, hoping that the stillness might help her gather her scattered thoughts. She walked slowly down the aisle, her boots thudding softly on the rubber mats. Willow lifted her head over the stall door the instant she saw Emma, her soft eyes glowing warmly in the dim light.

Emma exhaled a long, shaky breath. Willow always calmed her. Always. Just touching the mare's neck felt like placing her hand on something steady, something rooted deep into the earth.

"Morning, girl," Emma whispered, pressing her cheek to Willow's forehead. "I missed you."

Willow breathed against Emma's chest, warm and gentle.

Emma closed her eyes.

She needed this.

After everything that had happened the day before—Zoey's panic in the warm-up ring, Riley's refusal and humiliation, the raised jump, the tense conversation with Coach Sloane—Emma felt stretched thin. She felt like she was trying to hold everyone together with pieces of thread, her own heart tied up in knots.

And she was tired.

She was tired of carrying everyone's fear.

Tired of being the glue.

Tired of trying so hard to fix things she did not break.

She stroked Willow's neck, trying to let the warmth seep into her.

"Today is different," she whispered. "I need to do something different."

But she did not yet know what that something was.

Not until she heard footsteps behind her.

Cade.

Emma turned, surprised. "You are here early."

"So are you," Cade said, his voice low and quiet. He carried a small blue cooler bag in one hand. "Vet said Knightfall needs warm compresses twice a day. I wanted to get started before anyone else crowded the aisle."

Emma nodded. "Makes sense."

Cade looked down the aisle, then back at her. "You alright?"

The question caught Emma off guard. Cade had not asked her anything personal since he arrived. He had watched her ride. He had listened. He had observed. But he rarely asked.

Emma blinked. "I... I do not know."

Cade nodded as if he understood already. "A lot happened yesterday."

Emma swallowed. The memory of the raised jump flashed behind her eyes. "Yes."

Cade leaned against Knightfall's door, running a gentle hand along the gelding's cheek. Knightfall leaned into him with a soft, tired sigh.

"Coach told me she is investigating," Cade said.

Emma looked up sharply. "Investigating?"

"Yes," Cade said. "She does not think it was an accident either."

Emma's stomach twisted. "Do you think someone meant harm?"

Cade did not answer immediately. "I think someone acted without thinking. Maybe trying to prove something. Or trying to get attention. Or trying to show off. But whatever they meant, what happened was dangerous."

Emma hugged her arms around herself. "Riley thinks it was about her."

Cade's expression tightened. "Everything feels like it is about her right now."

Emma frowned. "What do you mean?"

Cade chose his words carefully. "She is angry. And scared. And she hides both by getting loud. That makes her look like the victim sometimes, even when she is not."

Emma bit her lip. "She did not deserve what happened."

"No," Cade agreed. "But Zoey did not deserve what happened in the warm-up. And Harper did not deserve to get stuck in the middle. And you..."

Emma looked up.

"You did not deserve to carry everyone's fear," Cade finished.

Emma's breath caught.

Cade looked at her with quiet understanding. "I see things. Even when people do not speak."

Emma lowered her gaze to the floor. "It feels like everything is falling apart."

"Then someone has to stop it," Cade said.

Emma blinked. "Who?"

Cade shrugged slightly. "Maybe the one who sees everyone clearly."

Emma's heart pounded.

He meant her.

But how could she? She was only one person. She was not the leader. She was not the loud one. She was not the brave one.

Or was she?

Before she could answer, a soft voice carried down the aisle.

"Emma?"

Zoey.

Emma turned to see Zoey standing near Daisy's stall, holding the lead rope with trembling hands. Zoey looked pale, her eyes still swollen from yesterday's tears. Her entire posture looked fragile, like a frightened bird.

"Can I talk to you?" Zoey whispered.

Emma nodded, walking closer. "Of course."

Zoey hesitated, glancing nervously toward Riley's stall even though Riley was not there yet. "I feel like everyone hates me."

Emma's heart cracked. "No one hates you, Zoey."

"It feels like they do," Zoey said, voice trembling. "Especially Riley. She looked at me yesterday like... like she wished I was not here."

Emma swallowed. "Riley is hurting. She is not angry at you."

Zoey shook her head. "She said she is tired of me being scared. She said I ruin things."

Emma took Zoey's hands gently. "Zoey. You did not ruin anything."

"She said I panic about everything. That everyone has to protect me. That I am too much work."

Emma's chest hurt. "Riley did not mean it."

"It does not matter if she meant it," Zoey whispered. "It still hurt."

Emma hugged her tightly. Zoey clung to her like she was holding onto something solid in a storm.

When Zoey pulled back, her eyes were shining with tears. "Emma. What if I do not belong here?"

Emma felt the world tilt. "Zoey. You do."

Zoey looked away. "I do not ride like you or Riley. I am not confident like Harper. I am scared all the time. I feel like I am slowing everyone down."

Emma took her shoulders gently. "Zoey. Riding is not about being fearless. It is about trying even when you are scared. You are one of the bravest people here."

Zoey shook her head. "No I am not."

"Yes you are," Emma said softly. "You got back on Daisy after the spook. You went into the ring yesterday even though you were terrified. You stayed on when Daisy stumbled. That takes courage."

Zoey wiped her eyes. "Riley thinks I am the problem."

"Riley is hurting," Emma repeated. "She is scared of failing. She feels embarrassed about yesterday. And she is scared of looking weak. That is why she lashes out."

Zoey frowned. "But why is she always angry at me?"

Emma sighed. She finally said the truth she had been holding inside for days. "Because you remind her of the parts of herself she does not want to admit. Riley gets scared too. She just hides it differently."

Zoey blinked. "She does?"

"Yes," Emma said. "Riley gets scared of losing. Scared of not being the best. Scared of people thinking she is not as strong as she pretends. And when you get scared, Zoey, she feels like she has to stay strong for you. But sometimes she cannot. And she does not know how to say that."

Zoey looked down. "I wish she would just talk to me. Instead of yelling."

Emma placed a hand on her back. "I know."

Zoey hesitated. "Can you talk to her?"

Emma felt her stomach drop.

Could she?

Was that her job? Was it fair to carry both Zoey's fear and Riley's anger? Was she strong enough to face Riley without making everything worse?

She did not know.

But Zoey looked at her with such desperate hope.

Emma exhaled. "I will try."

Zoey nodded gratefully.

Emma knew this moment mattered. The barn was a pressure cooker, the warm-up chaos still echoing in everyone's minds. If she did not step up now, the fracture in their group might become permanent.

She stroked Willow's neck again for strength.

Willow steadied her as always.

Emma straightened her shoulders.

Then she said softly, "I am going to find Riley."

Emma found Riley in the outdoor ring.

Riley had Ember on the lunge line, working her in a big, controlled circle. Ember's hooves pounded rhythmically into the icy footing, breath puffing into the cold air.

Riley's posture was stiff. Her jaw was clenched. Her hands shook slightly each time she snapped the whip gently toward Ember's hindquarters.

Emma approached carefully. "Riley?"

Riley did not look at her. "Not now."

Emma stepped closer. "I need to talk to you."

Riley exhaled sharply. "I said not now."

Emma stood tall. "I am not going away."

Riley spun to face her, eyes blazing. "What do you want, Emma? Do you want to lecture me again?"

Emma kept her voice calm. "No. I want to understand."

Riley's expression flickered. "Understand what?"

"Why you are so angry."

Riley scoffed. "You know why."

"No," Emma said softly. "I know you are angry at Zoey. And at the Silver Spur riders. And at yourself. But I do not know why you are angry at me."

Riley's face flushed. "I am not angry at you."

"You are," Emma said. "You have been for days. And I need to know why."

Riley looked away, clenching and unclenching her jaw.

Emma waited.

After a long moment, Riley whispered, "Because you always take Zoey's side."

Emma blinked. "Riley, I do not take sides."

"You do," Riley insisted. "Every time Zoey cries, you run to her. Every time she panics, you protect her. Every time she messes up, you fix it. What about me?"

Emma's breath caught. "Riley... I care about you."

"Do you?" Riley said, voice cracking. "Because it feels like you expect me to always be strong. Always be loud. Always be okay. But sometimes I am not. Sometimes I just want someone to help me the way you help her."

Emma stared at her, stunned.

All this time, Riley had not been angry at Zoey.

She had been hurting.

She had been hurting quietly, behind all the sharp words and loud frustrations.

Emma stepped closer. "Riley... I did not know."

"Of course you did not," Riley said with a hollow laugh. "Because I do not cry. I do not panic. I do not fall apart like Zoey. So no one notices when I am scared."

Emma's heart twisted painfully. "Riley. I am sorry."

Riley looked down, her voice small. "I hate being scared. I hate failing. I hate the feeling I got yesterday. Ember refused. In front of everyone. I felt... humiliated."

Emma inhaled. "Riley, everyone has bad rides. You are still an amazing rider."

"Not yesterday," Riley said in a whisper.

Emma placed a gentle hand on Riley's shoulder. "You do not have to be perfect to be part of us. You do not have to be strong all the time."

Riley's breath shook. "Then why do I feel like I do?"

Emma spoke softly. "Because you do not let anyone help you."

Riley finally met her eyes. For the first time, Emma saw fear there. Deep fear. Vulnerable fear.

And she saw how much Riley had been holding inside.

Emma took a breath. "Riley... Zoey is scared. But so are you. And so am I. We are all scared sometimes."

Riley looked down. "I do not know how to be scared."

Emma squeezed her hand. "Courage is not about not being scared. It is about admitting it."

Riley swallowed. "I do not want Zoey to think I hate her."

"Then tell her," Emma said gently. "She needs to hear it."

Riley nodded slowly. "Okay."

Emma exhaled. "And Riley... you can talk to me too. When you are scared."

Riley looked away, cheeks reddening. "That is embarrassing."

Emma smiled softly. "So what."

Riley snorted at that, the corner of her mouth twitching. "Okay. Maybe."

Emma felt warmth spread through her chest.

This, she realized, was courage.

Not jumping high. Not winning ribbons. Not riding flawlessly.

But facing the people you cared about.

Facing the truth.

Facing fear.

And she had just done it.

She had found her courage.

For real.

. . .

Later that afternoon, Emma gathered the girls around Willow's stall. The barn felt warmer, fuller, as if the tension had begun to thaw.

Zoey stood close to Daisy, looking nervous.

Harper stood between them, steady as always.

Riley approached hesitantly, Ember trailing behind her.

Emma nodded. "Let us talk."

Riley took a breath, then faced Zoey. "I am sorry."

Zoey's eyes filled instantly.

Riley continued, voice shaking, "I should not have yelled at you. Or blamed you. I was scared and embarrassed, and I took it out on you. That was wrong."

Zoey wiped her eyes. "I never wanted to make you feel alone."

Riley swallowed. "I know. And you do not. I just... forget how to ask for help."

Zoey stepped forward tentatively. "I can help you too. If you want."

Riley let out a small, breathy laugh. "Okay. Maybe I do."

Harper smiled softly. "Good."

Emma felt her heart swell.

The fracture between them had not vanished.

But it had begun to heal.

Together.

That evening, Emma returned to Willow's stall alone. The barn was quiet again, but it felt different this time. Less heavy. Less cold. More hopeful.

Emma brushed Willow's neck and whispered softly, "I found my courage today, girl."

Willow blinked slowly, pressing her forehead against Emma's shoulder.

Emma closed her eyes.

She knew winter was coming.

She knew the medal season was far from over.

She knew tensions would rise again.

But she had found something inside herself she had not known was there.

Courage.

She would need it.

Because change was coming.

And she was ready.

Chapter Ten

The morning of the medal final dawned with a sky so pale it almost seemed white. Frost glittered across the fields like someone had shaken silver dust over every blade of grass. The cold was not biting yet, but it carried the promise of what winter would soon bring. The kind of cold that settled deep into the ground and stayed there.

Emma stood at the barn's double doors, staring out at the shimmering landscape. Her breath curled into the air in thin wisps, rising slowly before fading away. She felt a strange mix of nerves and calmness in her chest, like her heart was a lake with one rippling line through its center.

Today was important.

Not because she wanted a ribbon. Not because the medal finals were a big deal.

But because she wanted to ride for the right reasons again.

She wanted to ride for Willow.

She wanted to ride for herself.

Willow nickered from her stall, her warm eyes reflecting the morning light. Emma walked to her, wrapping her arms around the mare's strong neck. Willow leaned into her, soft breath warming Emma's cheek.

"We got through a lot this week," Emma whispered. "I think we can handle today."

Willow flicked her ears and pressed her nose to Emma's shoulder.

Emma's stomach fluttered again. She wished confidence lasted longer. But every time she thought she had enough, something inside her wavered.

She stepped back and breathed in slowly. "We will be fine. We will."

Behind her, footsteps echoed in the aisle.

Riley appeared, already in her show pants, her face set with determination. But her expression no longer held the storm it had before. Instead, there was something steadier behind her eyes. Something more grounded.

"Morning," Riley said quietly.

Emma smiled. "Good morning."

Riley untied Ember, brushing the mare's shoulder. Her movements were softer than usual. More thoughtful.

Harper soon joined them, leading Chase carefully, her cheeks pink from the cold. "Coach Sloane is setting the final course now. She said it is harder than the last one."

Zoey stepped in moments later with Daisy, bundled in her winter coat, looking both nervous and excited. "I did a breathing exercise before coming. I think it helped."

Emma beamed at her. "You look ready."

Zoey flushed with pride.

Cade appeared at the far end of the aisle, Knightfall's halter slung over his shoulder. He could not ride today, but he still looked prepared, like he carried a role all the same. He nodded toward Emma. "Big day."

Emma nodded back. "Big day."

Coach Sloane strode into the aisle with a firm clap of her hands.

"Everyone listen up. Medal riders, meet me in the indoor in ten minutes for the course walk."

Her voice echoed through the barn, bouncing off the walls and settling low in Emma's stomach.

This was it.

The medal final.

No turning back now.

The indoor arena was colder than outside, a pocket of air that held the night's chill. But it felt focused. Intent.

The jumps were already set: a mix of small verticals, tight turns, a diagonal line with a bending approach, and a rollback toward a gate decorated with deep orange flowers. Nothing looked too scary, but nothing looked easy either.

Coach Sloane stood at the center, clipboard tucked under one arm. "This course is about precision. Not speed. Not bravery. Precision."

She pointed to the first two jumps. "Line one. You must decide your stride before you even start. If you come in too fast, you over-shoot. If you come in too slow, you chip the second fence."

Riley nodded, studying the line intensely.

Coach lifted her hand toward the diagonal. "The bending line here is critical. Look early. Turn early. Trust your horse."

Zoey swallowed hard.

Harper studied each jump with quiet focus, her fingers tracing the path from the air.

Emma checked her position relative to Willow. This was the part she loved most: imagining the ride before it began.

Coach finished with, "This is a test of how far you all have come. Show me what you know. And ride smart."

She dismissed them to tack up.

· · ·

Emma ran her fingers through Willow's mane once more, then tightened the mare's girth. Willow's coat glowed under the barn lights, freshly brushed and clean. Her muscles twitched lightly as Emma touched her shoulder.

"We can do this," Emma whispered.

Willow snorted as if agreeing.

Riley looked over from Ember's stall. "Your mare looks ready."

Emma smiled. "So does Ember."

Riley exhaled. "I hope so."

Harper led Chase out of his stall carefully. "Everyone remember to breathe."

Zoey giggled nervously. "Trying."

Cade walked by, giving Emma a small, supportive nod. "You will ride well."

Emma felt warmth spread through her chest. "Thank you."

Coach's voice carried down the aisle. "Riders, warm-up in five minutes."

Emma mounted Willow near the barn doors. Willow stepped lightly beneath her, eager and alert.

This was it.

The medal final.

The warm-up ring was busy, but nowhere near as chaotic as before. Coach Sloane had insisted on limited riders, strict spacing, and controlled trot circles. Emma breathed easier because of it.

Willow moved beautifully, her trot rhythmic and steady. Emma focused on their breathing together, matching her inhale to Willow's stride.

Riley rode Ember with a calm Emma had not seen in days. The mare responded well, her ears flicking back toward Riley in soft intervals.

Harper practiced smooth circles with Chase, giving him gentle encouragement.

Zoey guided Daisy in a slow, steady trot, her posture tighter than the others but far more confident than usual.

Emma felt proud of all of them.

When Coach Sloane finally called, "First rider to the gate," Emma's heartbeat thudded in her ears.

Emma rode to the rail beside Cade, who watched her quietly.

"You ready?" Cade asked.

Emma swallowed. "I hope so."

He tilted his head. "You are."

And strangely, she believed him.

She breathed slowly, then nudged Willow toward the gate.

Coach Sloane nodded. "Emma and Willow. You are on deck."

Emma walked Willow through the gate, her heart pounding steadily but not painfully.

For the first time in weeks, she felt something she had been missing.

Balance.

The arena fell silent when the announcer's voice rang out. "Next rider: Emma Carson on Willow."

Emma lifted her chin, breathed deeply, and guided Willow into a forward trot.

The arena felt enormous, the jumps tall and bright beneath the pale arena lights. But she forced her focus inward.

Just Willow.

Just the rhythm.

Just the course.

She approached the first line with a quiet, controlled trot. Willow transitioned smoothly into canter. Emma counted strides with silent precision, letting Willow stretch into the space naturally.

The first jump came toward them. Willow lifted beautifully, clearing it without hesitation.

Emma steadied her for the second jump, keeping her eyes up and steady.

Willow sailed over it, landing in perfect balance.

Emma's breath softened.

Next came the bending diagonal.

She looked early, turned early, exactly as Coach had instructed. Willow curved through the approach, her inside hind leg stepping underneath with power.

They reached the diagonal vertical.

Willow hesitated for half a heartbeat.

Emma softened her hands. "You got this."

Willow responded instantly, stretching her neck and lifting cleanly.

Emma felt her heart rise.

The rollback turn came next. She sat deep, guiding Willow around with her inside leg strong and sure.

The final gate stood at the far end, decorated with orange flowers.

Emma breathed as Willow approached.

She lifted her hands just slightly.

Willow soared.

The landing was smooth, strong, perfect.

Emma slowed Willow to a trot, heart glowing. She could hear clapping. Loud clapping. Harper. Zoey. Riley. Even Cade.

Her heart swelled with pride.

She had done it.

They had done it.

Riley watched from the gate, jaw tight but expression hopeful. Ember snorted beneath her, eager.

Coach Sloane nodded. "Your turn."

Riley squeezed her reins. "I am ready."

Emma moved aside, giving her space. Riley trotted Ember into the ring with a deep inhale.

The announcer called her name.

Riley set Ember into a steady canter.

At the first line, Ember rushed slightly, but Riley corrected her smoothly this time, using a quiet half-halt. Ember adjusted.

They cleared both fences.

Emma smiled softly.

The diagonal line approached. Riley looked early. Ember curved through the approach. They landed clean.

Then came the rollback.

Ember hesitated. Riley steadied her. Encouraged her.

And Ember listened.

They cleared the final gate with a bold, clean takeoff.

Riley slowed Ember and exited the ring with a smile she had not worn in days.

Emma stepped forward. "You did great."

Riley exhaled shakily, a quiet laugh escaping. "I did better than I expected."

Zoey added, "You were amazing."

Riley's smile softened. "Thank you."

A week ago, those words would have felt impossible.

But today was different.

Harper was next.

Her ride was clean, quiet, and beautifully controlled. Chase lifted over each fence with surprising grace, his ears forward and attentive. Harper's seat was steady, her hands soft, her mind completely focused.

Emma felt awe watching her.

Harper had always been overlooked, the steady one, the calm one. But today she shone. Her confidence was beginning to rise like a slow flame.

When she finished, Emma hugged her tightly. "You were incredible."

Harper blushed. "Thank you."

Emma meant it.

Zoey went last.

She guided Daisy in with small, careful breaths.

The first crossrail was perfect.

The second line was a little rough, but Zoey kept her seat.

When she reached the diagonal, Daisy looked uncertain. Zoey whispered encouragement. Daisy lifted over it with a small bobble, but Zoey stayed on.

Then the rollback.

Zoey's eyes widened.

Emma whispered from the gate, "Look early."

Zoey did.

Daisy rounded the turn.

The final jump approached.

Zoey inhaled. Daisy lifted. Landed.

Zoey finished with tears in her eyes.

She rode out trembling, but smiling.

"You did it," Emma whispered, hugging her.

"I really did," Zoey whispered back.

The judges took several minutes to finalize the results.

All four girls stood together near the rail, shoulders brushing, breaths syncing in the cold air. Cade stood beside them quietly.

Coach Sloane watched her riders with a rare, soft smile.

The announcer finally stepped into the ring.

"In fourth place... Zoey Bennett on Daisy."

Zoey gasped and beamed, hugging Daisy tightly.

"In third place... Riley Torres on Ember."

Riley grinned, cheeks pink with surprised pride.

"In second place... Emma Carson on Willow."

Emma felt warmth fill her entire body. Willow nudged her gently.

"And in first place... Harper Lin on Chase."

Harper froze.

Emma shrieked, grabbing her shoulders. "Harper! You did it!"

Riley laughed, hugging her.

Zoey wiped tears.

Harper stepped forward to accept her ribbon, completely overwhelmed.

The medal final ended not with rivalry, not with bitterness, but with pride.

Pride in each other.

Pride in themselves.

They walked back to the barn together, shoulder to shoulder, horses close, winter sunlight glowing behind them.

And though Emma did not win first, she felt something far more important settle inside her.

Courage.

Real courage.

Courage to face fear.

Courage to face friends.

Courage to be better.

The winter ahead would be hard. The storms would come. The indoor arena would shrink. Tempers would rise again.

But today?

Today they were a team.

Again.

And Emma knew they could weather anything.

Chapter Eleven

The afternoon after the medal final felt lighter than any day in weeks, as if something had finally unknotted inside Saddle Creek. Sunlight slid through the high arena windows, warm and golden despite the cold outside. Horses munched quietly on hay. Riders talked in soft voices. Even the air felt calmer.

Emma walked Willow slowly along the barn aisle, letting the mare cool down before untacking. Willow's ears flicked forward, relaxed after the long day. Emma stroked her neck, feeling the mare's warmth seep into her fingertips.

"You did amazing," Emma whispered.

Willow snorted happily and nudged her elbow.

Harper's laughter echoed down the aisle. She stood near Chase's stall, her first place ribbon still pinned proudly to her jacket. Every time she looked at it, her face glowed with disbelief.

"I cannot believe it," Harper murmured to Chase. "I really cannot."

Chase tossed his head proudly, as if he had known all along.

Zoey walked past with Daisy, smiling shyly. Her fourth-place ribbon fluttered at Daisy's bridle like a small flag of victory. She kept touching it gently, as if afraid it would disappear.

Riley was brushing Ember. Her movements were soft now, almost thoughtful. She hummed quietly, something Emma had not heard from her in a long time. Ember's ears stayed forward, relaxed.

It felt like the medal final had washed something clean in all of them.

Still, one shadow remained.

The raised jump.

The sabotage.

Or mistake.

Or whatever it had been.

Coach Sloane had not spoken about it again since their tense meeting in the arena. She had said she would handle it. And the girls had trusted her. But the mystery rested like a small stone in the bottom of Emma's stomach, refusing to dissolve.

She hoped today would bring answers.

Emma finished caring for Willow and hung up the mare's tack neatly. She had just finished sweeping the grooming area when she saw Coach Sloane step out of the office, her clipboard tucked under one arm and a folded paper in her hand.

Her expression was neutral, but her eyes were serious.

Emma exchanged a look with Harper, who stood nearby. Riley stopped brushing Ember. Zoey paused mid-reach toward Daisy's curry comb. Cade stepped out of Knightfall's stall, wiping his hands on his jeans.

Everyone instinctively moved toward Coach Sloane.

She waited until the aisle was clear and quiet, then gestured for the group to gather near the tack room benches.

Emma's heart thudded.

This was it.

Coach Sloane looked at each of them, her expression unreadable. "I have something important to tell you all."

The girls leaned in.

"About the altered jump."

Zoey inhaled sharply. Riley stiffened. Harper shifted closer to Emma. Cade crossed his arms but stayed silent.

Coach unfolded the paper. "I reviewed the security footage from yesterday."

Emma blinked. "There is security footage?"

Coach nodded. "In the indoor arena. It is a new system. I had forgotten it was active until this morning."

Riley's breath sped up. "And... what did it show?"

Coach looked down, then back up at them.

"The jump was raised by someone who thought they were correcting a mistake."

The girls stared.

"What?" Riley whispered.

Coach continued. "It was one of our youngest barn helpers. She thought someone set the jump too low. She had overheard a conversation about adjusting heights for the medal final. She assumed she was supposed to fix it."

Emma exhaled slowly.

Zoey touched her chest, relief washing over her face.

Harper whispered, "So it was not sabotage."

"No," Coach said firmly. "It was not sabotage. It was a mistake. A dangerous mistake, but a mistake."

Riley stared at the ground, her shoulders sinking. "So no one was trying to hurt me."

Coach's gaze softened. "No one at Saddle Creek would try to hurt you."

Riley swallowed hard.

"It was an accident," Coach repeated. "The helper apologized. I have talked with her and her parents. She understands how serious this was. And I will make sure it never happens again."

Zoey let out a slow, shaky breath.

Harper looked at Riley. "What a relief."

But Riley did not look relieved.

She looked ashamed.

Emma stepped closer. "Riley?"

Riley blinked hard, her eyes glistening. "I blamed people. I blamed everyone. I accused people in my head. I... I thought the worst."

Emma touched her arm. "When you are scared, your mind tells stories that are not true."

Riley choked out a small, humorless laugh. "Yeah. Big surprise."

Zoey stepped forward, her voice tiny. "Riley... it is okay."

Riley looked down. "It is not. I said things to you. Things I should never have said."

Zoey hesitated, then took a breath. "You were scared too."

Riley shook her head. "That is not an excuse."

Zoey moved closer, her eyes gentle despite the hurt she had carried all week. "Maybe not. But it helps me understand."

Emma watched something soften between them, something that had been tight and fragile for days.

Coach Sloane continued, "Fear can make good riders make poor decisions. It can make good friends say hurtful things."

Riley's eyes flicked toward Emma, then Harper, then Zoey. "I am sorry. For all of it."

Zoey nodded slowly. "I forgive you."

Harper smiled softly. "We all make mistakes."

Emma wrapped an arm gently around Riley's shoulders. "We do. That is why we learn together."

Riley let out a long breath, leaning into Emma's side for a moment before stepping back with a small, grateful smile.

Cade watched it all quietly, leaning against the stall door.

Emma turned to him. "You were right. Panic makes people assume the worst."

Cade shrugged slightly. "Happens to everyone. Even me."

Riley glanced at him. "Even you?"

Cade smirked. "Especially me."

Riley rolled her eyes, but her smile was genuine.

The tension in the aisle eased. The ugly weight of the sabotage fear dissolved completely, leaving behind only the faint ache of the week's arguments and the warmth of their growing forgiveness.

Coach Sloane clapped her hands lightly. "Now that the air is cleared, I want you all to hear something else."

The girls straightened.

Cade looked interested.

Coach Sloane continued, "The medal final judges gave very positive feedback on Saddle Creek's riders. They said our sportsmanship, even under pressure, was commendable."

Zoey brightened.

Harper smiled shyly.

Riley puffed out a proud breath.

Emma felt her chest warm.

"But," Coach added, raising one eyebrow, "they also said certain riders need to stop second-guessing themselves."

Emma's cheeks flushed.

Riley nudged her. "She means you."

Coach waited until Emma met her eyes. "Emma. You rode beautifully yesterday. But I saw your face after every fence. You questioned every choice."

Emma swallowed. "I just... wanted to do everything right."

"You did," Coach said. "But courage is not about perfection. It is about trust. Trust in your horse. Trust in your friends. Trust in yourself."

Emma felt Willow's warm breath in her memory. The mare had trusted her without hesitation.

"I will try," Emma whispered.

Coach smiled gently. "Trying is the first step."

Then she stepped back, nodding to the group. "Alright. Go cool down your horses. And enjoy the rest of your afternoon. You earned it."

Everyone dispersed with lighter steps.

But Coach Sloane lingered for just a moment longer, watching them with a thoughtful expression.

Emma wondered if she was already thinking about winter.

And the storms they would face next.

Later that afternoon, after the horses were fed and the sun dipped low behind the hills, the girls gathered around the hay room to help sweep the aisle. Cade stayed too, pushing a broom silently beside Emma. Zoey hummed softly. Harper organized tools. Riley grumbled about the cold but kept working.

Normal.

Peaceful.

Emma felt relief sink into her bones.

When the sweeping was nearly done, a sudden whinny broke through the air from the far end of the barn. A high, excited sound.

Emma turned. "Willow?"

No. It had come from past Willow's stall.

Hoofbeats echoed.

Then footsteps.

Coach Sloane appeared, holding something large and rolled under her arm.

"Everyone, gather in the lounge," she said.

The girls exchanged curious looks.

Even Cade raised an eyebrow.

They followed Coach inside.

The lounge was warm from the space heater in the corner, the smell of hot cocoa from the machine drifting through the air. Emma felt warmth slide over her shoulders as they all crowded inside.

Coach unrolled the sheet of paper and pinned it to the bulletin board.

A flyer.

A bright, crisp flyer with bold blue lettering.

Harper gasped.

Zoey pressed a hand to her mouth.

Riley stared.

Emma felt her heart flip.

Coach smiled. "Congratulations. Saddle Creek has been selected to host a special winter riding clinic. Invitations go out to our medal riders first."

Emma stepped closer.

The flyer read:

Winter Training Clinic with Guest Trainer Marissa Hart

A two-week intensive winter program focusing on confidence, precision, and rider-horse connection.

Emma's breath caught.

Marissa Hart was known everywhere. Former national medal champion. Published equestrian trainer. Known for tough critiques and brilliant breakthroughs.

Coach continued, "This is a huge opportunity. You will learn a great deal. It will be hard work. But I believe all of you are ready."

Riley's eyes widened. "Even me?"

Coach smiled. "Especially you."

Zoey whispered, "This is real?"

Harper whispered back, "It is real."

Emma stared at the flyer, her heartbeat thudding.

Winter at Saddle Creek.

Indoor arena.

Storms.

Frozen mornings.

Hard lessons.

New trainer.

New challenges.

New growth.

Coach Sloane looked at all of them. "This clinic will test you. But if you trust each other, you will come out stronger on the other side."

Emma swallowed.

She felt Willow's warmth at her back.

Harper's quiet confidence beside her.

Zoey's fragile courage rising.

Riley's fierce determination sharpening again.

Cade's steady presence in the background.

They were a team again.

They were ready.

Coach nodded once. "First snow is coming soon. And with it... new beginnings."

Emma felt the shift inside her.

Winter was coming.

But she was not afraid.

Not anymore.

Chapter Twelve

The morning after the winter clinic announcement felt different at Saddle Creek, as if the barn itself had inhaled deeply and now held something crisp and expectant in the air. Emma sensed it the moment she stepped out of the car. The sky was pale, washed in soft gray. The wind carried a new, sharper bite. The paddock fences were edged with a thin shimmer, as if frost was testing the world, deciding if it was time to settle in for good.

Willow called from her stall when Emma entered the barn, her warm voice echoing through the cold aisle. Emma hurried to her, tucking her hands into Willow's thick winter coat.

"Good morning," Emma whispered. "I think winter is really coming."

Willow nickered, pressing her soft muzzle into Emma's chest.

Emma looked down the aisle. Harper was sweeping near Chase's stall humming softly. Zoey sat on an overturned feed bucket brushing Daisy's tail, her breath forming little clouds. Riley leaned against Ember's stall door, arms crossed, her expression curious but calm.

Cade stood near Knightfall's stall, tucking a blanket over the gelding's shoulders. He looked more relaxed than he had in days.

Everything felt... almost normal again.

But beneath the calm, Emma felt something new. A growing anticipation. A prickle in the air like static.

Winter was nearly here.

And the clinic was coming with it.

Coach Sloane gathered them in the indoor arena after morning chores. She stood with her clipboard and the winter clinic flyer pinned behind her.

"Listen up," she said. "The clinic begins in two weeks. That gives us fourteen days to prepare your horses, your bodies, and your minds. Winter riding is different. It is colder. It is harder. It demands more focus."

Emma nodded. She remembered last winter's frozen reins and stiff fingers, though she had not been training as seriously back then. This would be different.

Coach continued, "For now, the clinic invitations go to medal riders. That means Emma, Harper, Riley, and Zoey."

Zoey inhaled sharply, almost dropping Daisy's lead rope. Harper hid a shy smile. Riley's eyes widened in surprise. Emma felt Willow shift happily beside her, sensing excitement.

Coach looked at them each in turn. "This clinic will challenge all of you. It will push your limits. And it will expose weaknesses. But if you trust your horses, if you trust each other, it will change you."

Riley raised a hand. "What about Cade?"

Everyone turned.

Cade blinked, clearly not expecting the spotlight.

Coach Sloane tapped her clipboard. "Cade is eligible too, depending on Knightfall's recovery. For now, he will participate in ground exercises and observation sessions."

Cade nodded silently.

Zoey whispered, "That is good. Knightfall will like learning from the ground."

Cade smirked slightly. "He likes anything that gets him attention."

Emma smiled. It felt good to hear humor between them again.

Coach closed her clipboard. "Before the clinic begins, we need to prepare for winter riding. That means more indoor sessions. More group warm-ups. More trust."

Riley groaned dramatically. "Indoor riding."

Coach raised an eyebrow. "You will survive."

Riley muttered, "Maybe."

Emma laughed under her breath. The indoor arena had always felt claustrophobic when crowded. And winter made everything louder: the echoes, the squeaks of saddles, the thump of hooves. She could already imagine the frustration that would come with it.

But she was ready.

For the first time this year, she felt ready for a challenge.

Coach dismissed them, and they all drifted toward the barn.

But something held Emma back.

The air.

The quiet.

The almost-snow smell the wind carried.

She looked at the large windows along the arena wall.

Something soft drifted down, slow and delicate.

A single flake.

Then another.

And another.

Emma's breath caught. "It is snowing."

Riley spun. "It is?"

Harper's smile spread. "Oh wow."

Zoey rushed to the glass, Daisy trotting behind her. "The first snow."

Cade stepped beside Emma. "Looks like winter did not want to wait."

The flakes fell gently at first. Dust-like. Light. Barely landing before melting. But within minutes, they thickened, swirling in small clusters across the paddocks.

Emma pressed her hand to the window.

The first snow at Saddle Creek.

Her heart fluttered.

This moment felt like a doorway.

Like stepping into the next chapter before she had even turned the page.

The snowfall turned the barn into a world of muffled sounds and soft edges. Horses whickered to each other, their warm breath fogging the cold air. The roof popped and creaked as the snow settled. The aisles filled with the scent of hay, wood, and winter.

Emma brought Willow into the indoor for a short ride. Harper and Chase joined her, followed by Zoey and Daisy. Riley came last, brushing snowflakes off Ember's mane after the mare stuck her head out of the barn doors like she wanted to taste the sky.

Cade walked Knightfall in hand, keeping him warm beneath a thick blanket. The gelding's eyes followed the girls curiously.

Coach Sloane monitored from the center.

"Walk only today," she instructed. "Let the horses adjust to the cold footing."

Emma guided Willow along the rail. The mare stepped confidently, ears flicking at the sounds of wind outside. Zoey rode beside her, posture tighter than earlier but determined.

The arena felt smaller already.

Harper's quiet voice floated through the air. "Feels different in here when it is cold."

Riley made a face. "Feels like a cardboard box."

Zoey giggled softly.

Emma nodded in agreement. "We are all going to have to get used to it."

Coach Sloane lifted her voice. "Riders, winter means less space and more noise. You must learn to keep your tempers low and your focus high. And that means working together."

Riley nudged Ember gently. "Did she mean that for me?"

Zoey whispered, "Maybe."

Riley sighed. "Probably."

Emma grinned. "Definitely."

Riley elbowed her playfully as she passed.

The reconciliation between them felt real now. Warm. Steady. Even Zoey's shoulders stayed looser around Riley. Harper's posture had relaxed. Cade seemed more at ease too, stepping closer to the group without hesitation.

Winter had begun, and somehow, it was bringing them together instead of pushing them apart.

When their ride ended, Emma dismounted and walked Willow out with long, mindful steps. Snow still drifted past the arena doors, thicker now, coating the ground in a blanket of soft white. The paddock fences shimmered like sugar lines across a frosted cake.

Emma inhaled deeply. The cold stung her lungs, but it made her feel alive.

Harper stood beside her, pulling Chase's cooler up around his neck. "Do you think the clinic is going to be really hard?"

Emma nodded. "Probably."

Zoey joined them. "I am nervous."

"Me too," Emma said.

Zoey looked surprised. "You are?"

Emma smiled. "Everyone is. Even Coach."

Zoey laughed softly. "Even Riley."

Riley walked by at that moment, Ember snorting beside her. "I heard that."

They all burst into laughter.

The sound warmed the cold aisle.

Cade brought Knightfall over. "The horses will like the first snow. They always do. But the second one? Not so much."

Zoey looked up. "Why the second one?"

Cade shrugged. "Because the novelty wears off and the ice shows up."

Riley groaned. "Do not mention ice."

Zoey whispered, "Ice scares Daisy."

Harper nodded. "Ice scares me too."

Emma smiled. "Then we stick together."

They all exchanged looks.

And it no longer felt like a fragile promise.

It felt solid.

Like something they could rely on.

Like something that could carry them through whatever winter threw at them.

After chores, Emma lingered by Willow's stall as the girls gathered their backpacks. She rested her hand on Willow's soft muzzle and watched the snow fall harder outside.

Riley stopped beside her. "Emma?"

"Yes?"

Riley looked hesitant, almost nervous. "I know everything is better now. And I am glad. But... I think winter is going to be hard on Zoey. And maybe on me. And maybe... on all of us."

Emma nodded. "It probably will be."

Riley sighed. "I do not want to mess things up again."

Emma squeezed her arm. "You won't. You know why?"

"Why?" Riley whispered.

"Because you are starting winter with honesty," Emma said. "Not pretending."

Riley smiled, small but real.

Harper joined them. "Coach wants us to come early tomorrow. Indoor group lesson."

Zoey groaned softly. "Indoor group lesson. First snow. This is going to be... interesting."

Riley smirked. "You mean crowded."

Harper raised an eyebrow. "You mean frustrating."

Zoey mumbled, "You mean terrifying."

Emma laughed. "All of the above."

But something in her chest glowed warm.

The barn felt unified again. Not perfect. Not fixed forever. But steady. Together.

And as the snow fell harder outside, swirling like a thousand tiny diamonds, Emma felt it:

The shift.

The doorway.

The beginning of something new.

Winter had arrived.

And with it, the next part of their journey.

That evening, as Emma stepped outside into the snow-covered world, she paused at the top of the driveway. The barn lights glowed behind her, warm against the cold evening sky. Horses whinnied softly inside. Laughter drifted faintly through the walls. The world smelled clean and cold.

Her breath curled into the sky.

Winter at Saddle Creek.

She could already feel it pressing forward.

The indoor riding frustrations.

The long hours in the cold.

The short tempers.

The sleepover planned to break up the darkness.

The storms waiting just beyond the hills.

The power outage that would come.

The night they would be tested together.

Harper's horse getting sick.

The trails buried in snow.

The friendships mended under frost.

The winter wonderland ride waiting at the end.

All of it waited.

Emma took a slow breath.

Then she whispered into the cold air,

"We are ready."

And with Willow beside her and her friends behind her, she truly believed it.

Chapter Thirteen

Thank you for riding with Emma, Willow, and all the Saddle Creek girls through another season of challenges, courage, and big horse-girl heart. Book 3 was a whirlwind of emotions. There were moments of fear, moments of frustration, moments when friendships wobbled, and moments when each rider had to choose who they wanted to be in the ring and beyond it.

Emma found courage she did not know she had.

Riley learned how to let people in.

Harper stepped into her quiet strength.

Zoey discovered she is braver than she believes.

Cade uncovered his place in their growing herd.

And Willow, Ember, Daisy, Chase, and Knightfall carried their riders through it all with steady hooves and loyal hearts.

But their journey is far from over.

Because winter is coming to Saddle Creek. Snow will fall. Ice will test every hoof and every friendship. Long indoor rides will push patience to the edge.

And the upcoming winter clinic will challenge the riders in ways they have not faced before.

Storms will come. Secrets will surface.

And one cold night, the horses will need their riders more than ever.

In **Book 4 - Winter at Saddle Creek**, the girls discover that courage looks different in the quiet, frozen months. Friendship feels different when the barn lights flicker in a storm. And sometimes the strongest moments happen in the stillness of winter.

Thank you for riding with Emma and Willow.

Saddle Creek is more magical because you are here.

Ready for the first snow?

Turn the page... the winter adventure awaits.

Wren Willowbrook